Alex Kava is the author of ten previous novels, eight of which feature FBI profiler Maggie O'Dell. A former PR director, Alex dedicated herself to writing full time in 1996. She lives in Nebraska, USA. Find out more at: www.alexkava.com.

Also by Alex Kava

Maggie O'Dell series
Black Friday
Exposed
A Necessary Evil
At the Stroke of Madness
The Soul Catcher
Split Second
A Perfect Evil
Damaged

Other fiction
Whitewash
One False Move

ALEX KAVA

HOTWIRE

sphere

SPHERE

Published in the United States in 2011 by Doubleday,
a division of Random House, Inc., New York
First published in Great Britain in 2011 by Sphere

A CIP catalogue record for this book
is available from the British Library.

Hardback ISBN 978-1-84744-342-7
Trade Paperback ISBN 978-1-84744-350-2

Printed and bound in Great Britain by
Clays Ltd, St Ives plc

Papers used by Sphere are from well-managed forests
and other responsible sources.

MIX
Paper from
responsible sources
FSC
www.fsc.org FSC® C104740

Sphere
An imprint of
Little, Brown Book Group
100 Victoria Embankment
London EC4Y 0DY

An Hachette UK Company
www.hachette.co.uk

www.littlebrown.co.uk

TO DEBORAH GROH CARLIN,
the wizard behind the curtain

THURSDAY, OCTOBER 8

ONE

———

NEBRASKA NATIONAL FOREST

HALSEY, NEBRASKA

Dawson Hayes looked around the campfire and immediately recognized the losers. It was almost too easy to spot them.

He could pretend he had some super radar in reading people, but the truth was he knew the losers because ... what was that old saying? It takes one to know one. It wasn't that long ago that he would have been huddled over there with them, wondering why he had been invited, sweating and waiting to see what the price of the invitation was.

He didn't feel sorry for them. They didn't have to show up. Nobody dragged them here. So anything that happened was sort of their own fault. Their price for wanting to be somebody they weren't. Admission to the cool club didn't come without some sacrifice. If they thought otherwise, then they really were hopeless losers.

At least Dawson accepted who he was. Actually he didn't mind. He liked being different from his classmates and sometimes he played up the part, purposely wearing all black on football Fridays when everyone else wore school colors. Being the geek got him noticed, even garnered an eye roll from Coach Hickman, who before Dawson started wearing black on Fridays hadn't bothered to remember Dawson's name.

At the beginning of the school year, during roll call for history class Coach would yell out "Dawson Hayes" and look around the entire room, over Dawson's head and sometimes straight at him. When Dawson raised his hand, Coach Hickman's eyebrows would dart up like the man would never in a million years have put a cool name like Dawson Hayes together with the pimpled face and the hesitant, skinny arm claiming it. Dawson didn't mind. He was finally starting to get noticed and it didn't matter how it came about.

Even now he knew the only reason for his continued invitation to these exclusive retreats in the forest was because Johnny Bosh liked what Dawson brought to the party. Tonight that something was burning a hole in Dawson's jacket pocket. He tried not to think about it. Tried not to think how earlier he had lifted it—that's right, lifted, borrowed, not stolen—from his dad's holster while the man slept on his one night off. His dad probably wouldn't care as soon as he heard Dawson was hanging with Johnny B. Okay, that wasn't true. His dad would be pissed. But wasn't he always encouraging Dawson to make friends, go do stuff that other kids were doing? In other words, be a normal teenager for a change.

Dawson thought that was part of his problem—he was too normal. He wasn't a superstar athlete like Johnny B or a tobacco-chewing cowboy like Trevor or a brainiac like Kyle, but just holding the Taser X26, with its lightweight, bright-yellow casing that fit perfectly in his hand, gave him a new identity and a sense of confidence. All he had to do was point and *wham*, there goes fifty thousand volts of electricity. And suddenly Dawson Hayes, the powerless, became powerful. He could control anyone and everyone. With this sleek piece of technology in the palm of his hand Dawson felt like he could do anything.

Okay, maybe it wasn't just the Taser. Maybe the salvia had a little something to do with it. He'd been chewing his wad for about fifteen minutes and he could already feel the effect. That was just one of the highlights of tonight.

Dawson looked for the camera hidden behind some low sweeping pine branches. Though it remained camouflaged he could see the green dot blinking only because he had helped Johnny set it up earlier, making sure the tripod blended in with the trees. No one else knew it was there. Being the geek in residence did have its advantages.

Dawson glanced around at the campground. They had stomped out an area for themselves in a secluded part of the pine forest where they probably shouldn't have a frickin' campfire. Johnny B said no one could see them from the road or the lookout tower, though it didn't matter. Both would be vacant. On one side was an open field, a swell of tall rolling grass separated by a barbed-wire fence. On the other side was the thick beginning of ponderosa pine. About ten yards away the Dismal River snaked by. Dawson could hear the water tonight, just a whisper running over the rocks.

They had left their vehicles about a quarter mile down in a deserted turnoff, a two-tire trail worn into the knee-high grass. They had to climb over a barbed-wire fence to enter the forest. The trek was only the first test of the night but Dawson thought it revealed quite a lot about tonight's guests. How they maneuvered and crawled over the sharp barbs showed just how capable they were. Whether they turned to help the next person get over or under the fence or if instead, they looked for assistance. Or worse, *expected* assistance.

That was another thing about Dawson that made him different from other kids his age. He liked watching how people reacted to each other, to their surroundings, and especially to the unpredictable. His generation had become mindless zombies, mimicking and copying each other, caught up in their own little worlds of *what is* rather than *what if*. That was probably what interested him most about Johnny's experiments.

There were only seven of them here tonight and yet they still grouped together in their cliques. Johnny was surrounded by the babes, Courtney and Amanda. Tonight even

Nikki had inserted herself into the cool clique, which disappointed Dawson. He had hoped that Nikki would be better than that. All three girls looked like they were hanging on every one of Johnny's words, laughing and tossing their hair back then tilting their chins in that way girls do to show their interest.

That was okay. Johnny was good at looking like it was his club, his party. Quarterback, homecoming king, he was charming but with just enough of a badass attitude that nobody challenged him. Being Johnny's friend was safer than being someone who annoyed him.

Dawson wasn't quite sure why Johnny wanted the Taser. He didn't need it. Johnny exuded confidence, even in those silly cowboy boots. Kids called him Johnny B and it was the coolest nickname. Dawson had even heard Mr. Bosh call out "Johnny be good" at one of the football games and then the man laughed like he expected just the opposite from his son and that it was perfectly okay with him.

The first flash of light came without a sound. Everyone turned but only briefly.

The second flash crackled overhead. Dawson thought it might be lightning but it blurred into blue and purple veins that spread over the treetops like a crack in the twilight sky.

Dawson heard "oohs" and "aahs," and smiled to himself. They're tripping out, enjoying the fireworks. He probably was, too.

He hadn't used salvia before but Johnny B said it was better than anything from the family medicine cabinet and way more potent than regular weed. Johnny said it was like "rock'n'roll fireworks squeezing your brain, convincing you that you could fly."

Dawson thought the stuff looked harmless. Green, the color of sage, with wide leaves and similar to something he'd find in his mom's old flower beds.

God, he missed his mom.

Dawson squashed some more of the plant into a tight wad and stuck it into his mouth between his gum and cheek like chewing tobacco, no longer wincing at the bitter flavor.

Johnny had called the plant "Sally-D" and told them that the Indians used it for healing. "It'll clear your sinuses, clean out your guts, soothe your aches, and erase the static in your brain."

However, he also sounded this excited last week when he had them all snort the OxyContin he'd crushed into fine particles. He had been able to confiscate only two of the pills from his mom's medicine cabinet so the effects—when crushed and spread out among a dozen kids—didn't quite live up to Johnny's promises. But here he was, once again, sounding like an infomercial, working his magic and getting them to give the new drug a try in the hopes of feeling good and being cool.

Less than a minute after Dawson's second hit he felt light-headed, a pleasant mind-tickling buzz that disconnected him from the others as he watched them stumble and laugh and point at the sky. It was like he was watching from another room, in slow motion from a faraway galaxy right outside his bedroom window.

There was a deep bass rhythm pounding, pounding, pounding at the base of his skull. Tree branches started to sway. Their trunks multiplied, by twos then threes.

That's when he saw the red eyes.

They were hidden in the bush, back behind Kyle and Trevor, right behind Amanda.

Fiery dots watched, darting back and forth.

How could the others not see this creature?

Dawson opened his mouth to warn them but no sound came out. He lifted his arm to point but he didn't recognize his hand, yellow and green, almost fluorescent in the flashing strobe light that came out of the treetops. Waves of purple and blue crackled through the branches.

That's when Dawson first smelled the heat. Almost like someone had left on a hot iron for too long. Then suddenly the smell was stronger, reminding him of scorched hot dogs on an open campfire—black, crispy, burned meat. Then he remembered they hadn't brought any food.

The sensation started as a tingle. Static electricity traveled the airwaves. The others felt it, too. They weren't "oohing" and "aahing" anymore. Instead, they stumbled, heads tilted upward, searching the treetops.

Dawson looked back at the brush for the fiery red eyes. *Gone.*

His head swiveled. He could hear a mechanical click in his head like his eyes had become a machine. Each blink scraped like a camera shutter. Every movement ticked and echoed in his head. His nostrils flared, sucking in air that singed his lungs. A metallic taste stuck in his throat.

The next flash of light sizzled, leaving a tail of live sparks.

This time Dawson heard shouts of surprise. Then cries of pain.

Suddenly the fiery red eyes came running out of the brush, racing straight at Dawson from across the campsite.

Dawson raised his arm, aimed the Taser, and pulled the trigger.

The creature reeled back, fell, and sprawled in the leaves, kicking up glowing stars that shot out of a bed of pine needles. Dawson didn't wait for the creature to spring to its haunches. He turned and started running, or at least his legs did. The rest of him felt carried, shoved into the forest by a force stronger than his own feet.

It was all he could do to raise his arms and protect his face from the branches. They tore at his clothes and slashed his skin. He couldn't see. The pounding at the base of his skull drowned out all other sound. The flashes were hot and bright behind him. In front of him, total dark.

He hit the wire hard. The jolt of electricity knocked him off his feet. He stumbled and felt his skin pierced and caught like a fish on a thousand hooks. The pain wrapped arrows around his entire body and stabbed him from every direction.

By the time Dawson Hayes hit the ground, his shirt was slick with blood.

TWO

———

"There's no blood?" Special Agent Maggie O'Dell tried not to sound out of breath.

She was annoyed that she was having trouble keeping up. She was in good shape, a runner, and yet the rolling sand dunes with waves of tall grass made walking feel like treading water. It didn't help matters that her escort was a good ten inches taller than her, his long legs accustomed to the terrain of the Nebraska Sandhills.

As if reading her mind, State Patrol Investigator Donald Fergussen slowed his pace for her to catch up with him. She thought he was being polite when he stopped, but then Maggie saw the barbed-wire fence that blocked their path. He'd been a gentleman the entire trip, annoying Maggie because she had spent the last ten years in the FBI quietly convincing her male counterparts to treat her no differently than they'd treat another man.

"It's the strangest thing I've ever seen," he finally answered when Maggie had almost forgotten she'd asked a question. He'd been like that on the drive from Scottsbluff, giving each question deliberate consideration then answering with genuine thought. "But yeah, no blood at the scene. None at all. It's always that way."

End of explanation. That had also been his pattern. Not just a man of few words but one who seemed to measure and use words like a commodity.

He waved his hand at the fence.

"Be careful. It could be hot," he told her, pointing out a thin, almost invisible wire that ran from post to post, about six inches above the top strand of four separate barbed wires.

"Hot?"

"Ranchers sometimes add electric fencing."

"I thought this was federal property."

"The national forest's been leasing to ranchers since the 1950s. It's actually a good deal for both. Ranchers have fresh pastures and the extra income helps with reforestation. Plus grazing the land prevents grass fires."

He said all this without conviction, simply as a matter of fact, sounding like a public service announcement. All the while he examined the wire, his eyes following it from post to post as he walked alongside it for several steps. He kept one hand out, palm facing her, warning her to wait as he checked.

"We lost five thousand acres in '94. Lightning," he said,

his eyes following the wire. "Amazing how quickly fire can sweep through the grass out here. Luckily it burned only two hundred acres of pine. That might not mean much somewhere else, but this is the largest hand-planted forest in the world. Twenty thousand of the ninety thousand acres are covered in pine, all in defiance of nature."

Maggie found herself glancing back over her shoulder. Almost a mile away she could see the distinct line where sandhill dunes, covered by patches of tall grass, abruptly ended and the lush green pine forest began. After driving for hours and seeing few trees, it only now occurred to her how odd it was that a national forest even existed here.

He found something on one of the posts and squatted down until he was eye level with it.

"Most forest services say fire can be good for the land because it rejuvenates the forest," he continued without looking at her, "but here, anything destroyed would need to be replanted. That's why the forest even has its own nursery."

For a man of few words he now seemed to be expending them, but maybe he thought it was important. Maggie didn't mind. He had a gentle, soothing manner and a rich, deep voice that could narrate *War and Peace* and keep you hanging on his every word.

At first introductions, he had insisted she call him Donny and she almost laughed. In her mind the name implied a boy. His bulk and weathered face implied just the opposite. His smile did have a boyish quality accompanied by dimples, but the crinkles at his eyes and the gray-peppered hair telegraphed a more seasoned investigator. But then all he had to do was take off his hat—like he did now so the tip of his Stetson didn't touch the wire—and the cowlick sticking straight up at the beginning of a perfectly combed parting brought back the boyish image.

"Ranchers hate fire." Donny paused to take a closer look at the wood post immediately in front of him. He tilted his head and craned his neck, careful not to touch the fence or the post. "The ranchers shake their heads at rejuvenation. The way they look at it, why destroy and waste all that valuable feedstock."

Finally he straightened up, put his hat back on, and announced, "We're okay. It's not hot." But then he tapped the wire with his fingertips like you check a burner to make sure it's been turned off.

Satisfied, his huge hands grasped between the barbs, one on each strand of the middle two, separating a space for her.

"Go ahead," she told him.

She had to wait for him to shift from a gentleman to a fellow law enforcement officer. It took a few minutes for his blank stare of protest to disappear. Then he finally nodded and readjusted his grip to the top two strands instead of the middle two so he could accommodate his longer legs.

Maggie watched closely how he zigzagged his bulk between the wires without catching a single barb. Then she mimicked his moves and followed through, holding her breath and wincing when she felt a razor-sharp barb snag her hair.

On the other side of the fence they continued walking through the knee-high prairie grass. The sun had started to slip below the horizon, turning the sky a gorgeous purple-pink that seeped into the twilight's deep blue. Out here in the open field, Maggie wanted to stop and watch the kaleidoscope effect.

She caught herself tucking away details to share later with Benjamin Platt, only she'd relate them in cinematic terms. "Think of John Wayne in *Red River*," she would tell him when she described the landscape. It was a game they played with each other. Both of them were classic-movie buffs. In less than a year what started as a doctor-patient relationship had turned into a friendship. Except recently Maggie found herself thinking about Ben as more than a friend.

She stumbled over the uneven ground and realized the grass was getting thicker and taller. She struggled to keep up with Donny.

He was a giant of a man, wide neck and barrel chest. Maggie thought he looked like he was wearing a Kevlar vest under his button-down shirt, only there was no vest, just solid, lean muscle. He had to be at least six feet five inches tall, maybe more because he seemed to bend forward slightly at the waist, shoulders slumped as if walking against a wind, or perhaps he was uncomfortable with his height.

Maggie found herself taking two steps to his one, sweating despite the sudden chill. The sinking sun was quickly stealing all the warmth of the day and she wished she hadn't left her jacket back in Donny's pickup. The impending nightfall seemed only to increase Donny's long gait.

At least she had worn comfortable flat shoes. She'd been to Nebraska before so she thought she had come prepared, but her other visits had been to the far eastern side near Omaha, the state's only metropolitan city, which sprawled over a river valley. Here, within a hundred miles of the Colorado border, the terrain was nothing like she expected. On the drive from Scottsbluff there had been few trees and even fewer towns. Those villages they did drive through took barely a few minutes and a slight decrease of acceleration to enter and exit.

Earlier Donny had told her that cattle outnumbered people and at first she thought he was joking.

"You've never been to these parts before," he had said rather than asked. His tone had been polite, not defensive when he noticed her skepticism.

"I've been to Omaha several times," she had answered, knowing immediately from his smile that it was a bit like saying she had been to the Smithsonian when asked if she had seen Little Bighorn.

"Nebraska takes nine hours to cross from border to border," he told her. "It has 1.7 million people. About a million of them live in a fifty-mile radius of Omaha."

Again, Donny's voice reminded Maggie of a cowboy poet's and she didn't mind the geography lesson.

"Let me put it in a perspective you can relate to, no

disrespect intended." And he had paused, glancing at her to give her a chance to protest. "Cherry County, a bit to the northwest of us, is the largest county in Nebraska. It's about the size of Connecticut. There are less than six thousand people in nearly six thousand square miles. That's about one person per square mile."

"And cattle?" she had asked with a smile, allowing him his original point.

"Almost ten per square mile."

She had found herself mesmerized by the rolling sandhills and suddenly wondering what to expect if she needed to go to the bathroom. What was worse, Donny's geography lesson only validated Maggie's theory, that this assignment—like several before it—was yet another one of her boss's punishments.

A couple of months ago Assistant Director Raymond Kunze had sent her down to the Florida Panhandle, smack-dab in the path of a category-5 hurricane. In less than a year since he officially took the position, Kunze had made it a habit of sending her on wild-goose chases. Okay, so perhaps he was easing up on her, replacing danger with mind-numbing madness.

This time he had sent her to Denver to teach at a weekend law enforcement conference. The road trip to the Sandhills of Nebraska was supposed to be a minor detour. Maggie specialized in criminal behavior and profiling. She had advanced degrees in behavioral psychology and forensic science. Yet it had been so long since Kunze allowed her to work a real crime scene she wondered if she would remember basic procedure. Even this scene didn't really count as a crime, except perhaps for the cows.

Now as they continued walking, Maggie tried to focus on something besides the chill and the impending dark. She thought, again, about the fact that there was no blood.

"What about rain?"

Almost instinctively she glanced over her shoulder. Backlit by the purple horizon, the bulging gray clouds looked more ominous. They threatened to block out any remaining light. At the mention of rain, Donny picked up his pace. Anything more and Maggie would need to jog to keep up.

"It hasn't rained since last weekend," he told her. "That's why I thought it was important for you to take a look before those thunderheads roll in."

They had left Donny's pickup on a dirt trail off the main highway, next to a deserted dusty black pickup. Donny had mentioned he asked the rancher to meet them but there was no sign of him or of any other living being. Not even, she couldn't help but notice, any cattle.

The rise and fall of sand dunes blocked any sign of the road. Maggie climbed behind him, the incline steep enough she caught herself using fingertips to keep her balance. Donny came to an abrupt stop, waiting at the top. Even before she came up beside him she noticed the smell.

He pointed down below at a sandy dugout area about the size of a backyard swimming pool. Earlier he had referred to something similar as a blowout, explaining that these areas were where wind and rain had washed away grass. They'd continue to erode, getting bigger and bigger if ranchers didn't control them.

The stench of death wafted up. Lying in the middle of the sand was the mutilated cow, four stiff legs poking up toward the sky. The animal, however, didn't resemble anything Maggie had ever seen.

THREE

At first glance, Maggie thought the scene looked like an archaeological dig revealing some prehistoric creature.

The cow's face had been sliced away leaving a permanent macabre grin, jawbone and teeth minus flesh. The left ear was missing while the right remained intact. The eyeballs had been plucked clean, down to the bone, wide sockets staring up at the sky. Though the carcass lay half on its side, half on its back, stiff legs straight out, its neck was twisted, leaving the head pointing nose-up. Maggie couldn't help thinking the animal had been trying one last time to get a look at who had done this to her.

Maggie guessed at the gender. Anything that would identify the cow as male or female had been cut away and was gone. And again, there was no blood. Not a speck or a splatter. What had been done was precise, calculated, and brutal. Still, she needed to ask.

"Forgive the obvious question," she said carefully,

treating this like any other crime scene, "but why are you absolutely certain predators did not do this?"

"Because bobcats and coyotes don't use scalpels," a new voice said from behind her. "Not the last time I checked."

This was obviously the rancher they were meeting. The man came down the hill letting his cowboy boots slide in the sand, picking up his feet over tufts of grass then sliding down some more. Even in the fading light, he maneuvered the terrain without needing to look. He wore jeans, a base-ball cap, and a lightweight jacket—the latter something Maggie was starting to covet.

"This is Nolan Comstock," Donny said. "He's been graz-ing his cattle on this parcel—how long has it been, Nolan?"

"Near forty years for me. And I've never lost a cow that looks like this one. So I hope you aren't gonna waste my time and yours just to tell me a fucking coyote did this."

"Nolan!" Donny's usually calm, smooth voice now snapped. Maggie saw his neck go red; then, correcting him-self, he changed his tone and said, "This is Maggie O'Dell from the FBI."

Nolan raised a bushy eyebrow and tipped back his cap. "Didn't mean any disrespect, ma'am."

"I'd prefer you didn't use that term."

"What? The FBI doesn't swear these days?"

"No. I mean 'ma'am.'"

She saw the men exchange a look but they'd missed her attempt at humor. She ignored them and squatted in front of the carcass, making sure she was upwind. She hadn't come all this way to get into a pissing contest between an old rancher who couldn't care less about a woman FBI agent and a law officer who insisted he notice.

"Walk me through the details," she said without looking back at either man. They were losing light and patience would soon follow.

"It's like all the others." It was Donny who answered. "Eyes, tongue, genitals, left ear, sides of the face—"

"Left ear," she interrupted. "Is that significant?"

"ID tags usually go in the left," Nolan said.

When Maggie didn't respond, Donny continued. "All are precision cuts. No blood from the incisions. It's like they're completely drained. But there's no footprints. No tire tracks."

"And no animal tracks," Nolan added. "Not even hers. Her calf's been bleating. No way she wandered off without it. The rest of the herd's about half a mile west of here. I'm guessing she'd been down here two days, and yet, take a look. Vultures haven't even touched her."

And no flies or maggots, Maggie noticed but didn't mention. Without blood it would take longer for the carcass to attract the regular vermin that usually invaded.

Maggie stood, walked to the other side of the animal, and squatted down again. Several minutes passed as she let her eyes scan and examine. She noted the complete silence, the almost reverent quiet of her hosts. She glanced up at both men who remained side by side watching from a good fifteen feet back like spectators, waiting expectantly.

"So is this where I'm supposed to hear the theme music from the *X-Files*?" she asked.

Neither man blinked or smiled.

Seconds passed before Nolan turned to Donny and said, "*X-Files*? What the hell is that?"

"It was a TV show."

"TV show?"

"It was a joke," Donny explained, recognizing it as such but he still didn't smile.

"A bad joke," she added as way of an apology.

"You think this is a joke?"

It was too late. She'd struck a nerve. Nolan bared yellow, coffee-stained teeth in a sarcastic smile accompanied by narrowed dark eyes.

"This is no prank," he told her. "And this isn't the only one. By my count, this is number seven in three weeks. And just here on forest property. That doesn't include what we're hearing about over the border in Colorado. And it doesn't count those that haven't been reported. I know at least one rancher who found a Black Angus steer last month but he won't report it on account of insurance won't pay on cattle mutilations."

"I didn't mean to offend you," Maggie said. "I just meant that it is very strange."

"That other guy, Stotter"—and this time Nolan was addressing Donny—"he seemed to believe it was UFOs, too. There's no way to catch these people. Hell, I don't even know if it is people according to you experts. All I'm saying is that I'm gettin' tired of lame explanations and excuses."

"So what do you think it is?" Maggie asked as she stood to face him.

The old rancher looked surprised that she'd want his opinion.

"Me personally?"

She nodded and waited.

Nolan glanced up at Donny, almost as if what he was about to say might offend the state patrolman.

"I think it's our tax dollars at work."

"You think it's the government," Donny said. "Because of the lights and the helicopters."

"Helicopters?" Maggie asked.

"Folks out here are used to seeing strange lights in the night sky. Some claim they've seen helicopters," Donny explained. "There are a couple of ranchers in Cherry County who use helicopters to check their herds."

"These are no ranchers' helicopters." Nolan shook his head. "Those make noise. I'm talking black ops helicopters."

"And others have claimed they've seen alien spacecraft," Donny added with a tone that was meant to nullify both claims.

"Followed by fighter jets," Nolan said, not paying attention to Donny who now rolled his eyes and crossed his arms over his massive chest.

"That was only one time," Donny came back with. "We're smack-dab between NORAD and STRATCOM," he told Maggie. Then to Nolan he said, "There wasn't any verification from either military base on fighter jets in this area."

"Of course not."

Maggie stood back and watched them. There was obviously a lot of information left out of her x-file. Nolan pinned her down with his eyes.

"So maybe you can tell us," he said. "Is there some classified government project?"

She looked back at the butchered animal, noticing how the open wounds still looked raw in the fading light. Then she met the rancher's eyes.

"What makes you think the government would tell me?"

That's when the two-way radio clipped to Donny's belt started squawking.

Even in the Nebraska Sandhills, Maggie recognized the codes. Something was wrong. Very wrong.

FOUR

TEN MILES ON THE OTHER SIDE

OF THE NATIONAL FOREST

Wesley Stotter struggled with the tailgate of his 1996 Buick Roadmaster. The wireless microphone stabbed at his Adam's apple but remained attached to the collar of his flannel shirt. He was fully aware that he was live streaming yet he was caught speechless, his eyes glued to the sky.

Lights exploded in the distance. Blue and white moving up then down, right to left like no aircraft Stotter had ever seen. But he *had* seen similar lights before.

"Son of a bitch," he said out loud, suddenly not caring if the FCC slapped him with another fine. They had been trying to run him off the air for more than a decade but Stotter was used to people trying to shut him up. As a result, UFO Network—his grassroots organization dedicated to proving the existence of extraterrestrial beings and the government's attempt to cover it up—only grew stronger. He had built a loyal following of thousands. Tonight his radio and webcam audiences were in for a real treat.

"You will not believe this, my friends," he said, adjusting the wireless mic as he pulled at the car's tailgate. It finally dropped open with a crack, metal scraping on metal. Without looking, he found a duffel bag and his fingers frantically searched inside the bag until he found the camera.

"More lights in the night skies," Stotter began his narration while trying to calm his shaky fingers. Sometime in the last several years arthritis had started to set in, making everything a challenge. He wiped his sweat-slick palms, one at a time, on his khakis and continued to fumble with the buttons on the camera.

"Friends, I'm in the Nebraska Sandhills tonight, just outside of Halsey and about ten miles east of the national forest. Holy crap! There they go again."

The lights made a sharp pivot and headed straight toward Stotter. There were three, like bright stars in tight formation, moving independently but together as a unit.

He swung the camera up, relieved to see the viewfinder open and the night-vision function on. The Record button was a bright red. It took every bit of concentration for Stotter to steady his hands.

"Those of you listening who are Stottercam subscribers, you should be getting a shaky view of this incredible sight. For the rest of you let me attempt to describe it. The lights are going to come directly over me. Friends, it looks like

Venus and two companions—that's the size and brightness—only they're moving together through the sky, slowly now. But just a few seconds ago they were shooting up and down, independent of each other. Almost like polar opposites."

Stotter had been chasing lights in the night sky since he was old enough to drive. As a boy he had listened to his father tell stories about his days in the army. John Stotter had been stationed at the army's guided missile base at White Sands shortly after the end of World War II where a classified program did test launches of German V-2 rockets. Fifty miles to the east was a nuclear-testing facility at Alamogordo and also nearby was the army's 509th airfield just outside Roswell, New Mexico.

The story Wesley Stotter enjoyed the most was the one his father told about being on night patrol July 1, 1947, when he watched an alien spaceship fall out of the night sky and slam into the desert. John Stotter had been one of the first to arrive at the crash site. His description of what he saw that night could still raise the hair on Wesley's arms.

Wesley Stotter would be sixty next year and as a self-professed expert in UFOs he had seen many strange things, but he had yet to experience anything like his father's close encounter.

Maybe tonight was that night.

The lights stopped before reaching Stotter and hovered over an area of sand dunes. Somewhere in between Stotter knew that the Dismal River snaked through pasture land. The water separated grazing fields from the national forest. Stotter contemplated driving closer but there were no roads. Only sandy, bumpy cattle trails in the tall grass. He couldn't risk spinning the tires of the Stottermobile and getting stuck in a blowout or scraping off the muffler again like he did two weeks ago.

He loved his Roadmaster. The wood panel had one small scruff—that was all—and the interior was still in pristine condition. Every year he told himself maybe he should get an off-road vehicle, but money was tight these days. His syndicated radio gig didn't pay much and his UFO Network depended on membership fees.

Stotter missed the days of the Comet Hale-Bopp and cults like Heaven's Gate stirring up the public. How could you beat or replicate young followers putting on their Nike high-tops, tightening plastic bags over their heads, then lying down and waiting for the spacecraft traveling in the tale of the comet to come and whisk them away to their greater destiny? No one could make up crap that good.

These days the Internet allowed UFO junkies to get their fill 24/7. They didn't have to depend on Wesley Stotter. But just as the economy was cyclical, so was alien fascination. The more unsure and chaotic the world became, the more people started looking for something to blame their fears on. So Stotter's webcam investment was giving Stottermania a second life.

He continued his narration for his radio audience,

slipping in his characteristic tidbits of history and folklore, the kinds of things his cult following gobbled up.

"This is sacred land," he said in a soft reverent tone and yes, sure, a bit theatrical. "The Cheyenne hid in these valleys in between sand dunes, surviving a brutal fall and winter in 1878–79. Soldiers from Fort Robinson hunted them down, wanting to imprison them. When that didn't work, they slaughtered more than sixty men, women, and children right here in these valleys.

"They say the Dismal River ran red with their blood. So you might, indeed, call this hallowed ground. Coincidence that another civilization would hone in and choose the sky over this same valley where the energy of Cheyenne spirits still rise up at twilight? Nope. I don't think so."

Stotter's hands were steady now, the camera tracking the lights. How many minutes had it been? They had remained stationary for so long that anyone first seeing them might simply think they were stars.

Then just as suddenly as they had appeared, they shot out, so quickly Stotter couldn't move the camera fast enough. They streaked above him, shooting up and out, like meteors, only no jet stream, no cosmic dust was left behind. Without a sound they were gone.

Stotter stayed plastered to the side of the car where he had leaned to hold himself up. His head tilted back, his face to the sky, mouth gaping. Only now did he notice his flannel shirt was glued to his sweat-drenched back. His beard itched and his balding scalp tingled. There was a ringing in his ears and it felt like an electrical surge had passed through him.

He glanced back, expecting the lightning to be close. Instead the thunderheads stayed on the horizon. In the twilight they looked more like mountains than clouds.

He signed off and managed to reach up and click off his microphone. That's when he heard a voice saying "... asking all emergency personnel ..."

It was his police scanner. Had they seen the lights?

"... reporting injuries. Southwest side of the forest off Highway 83."

Wesley Stotter spun around to look at the sky over the national forest. It was in the opposite direction of where he had seen the lights. But it had to be related.

He checked his watch. Then he rammed his equipment back into the duffel bag. Slammed the tailgate, making three attempts before it stuck in place.

He was close enough that he could be one of the first to arrive. He would witness the damage before anyone had a chance to cover it up this time.

FIVE

Maggie recognized the smell from another time, another place. Scorched flesh, singed hair. This is what her father smelled like lying inside his casket. He had been a firefighter, killed in the line of duty. Maggie would never forget the smell of his burned flesh, despite the plastic wrapped around his arms and legs.

The odor was alarming, but it was the moans—soft, wounded cries in the darkness—that unnerved Maggie the most. She wasn't a first responder. Though she knew CPR, most of her victims didn't need it. Usually, by the time Maggie arrived, they were dead.

Slices of light from high-powered flashlights caught the huddled figures crouching, hiding. Leaves swirled and skittered away like frightened animals.

Maggie would never forget the looks on their faces. Eyes wide. Lips trembling. Some of them mumbled incoherently. Hands and arms flayed in front of them, jerking under the flashlight beams like stoned dancers under a revolving disco ball.

Maggie had put on her leather jacket before leaving the pickup but her chill came from within. The darkness inside the forest disarmed her, swallowing up everything that the flashlights missed.

The canopy of branches became a moving ceiling, creaking and swaying. Gaps allowed a view of black sky. Once in a while the full moon pierced through the cloud cover—the result a brief and startling streak of sudden illumination.

A tall, thin forest ranger named Hank guided Maggie and Donny. He had met them at the main campground, telling them they wouldn't be able to get a vehicle down to the site.

"You're the first to arrive," he had said with such relief Maggie found herself hoping Donny would know what to do with the injured. Her specialty—heaven forbid it was called on—would be dealing with those who could afford to wait.

"Damn, it's steep," Donny kept repeating.

Maggie was thinking the same thing as she followed him down an overgrown trail, feeling more than seeing, grabbing branches before they whipped into her face, missing a few and feeling the sting. How the hell were they going to get the injured back up this path?

By the time the three of them reached a flat clearing, they were breathing hard. Maggie felt sweat trickle down her back despite the cold.

"We're here to help," Donny called out so low and gentle

Maggie wondered if anyone heard him. "We need to get some light down here, Hank."

"I've got one of my guys bringing down strobes with a mobile generator."

The dispatcher's details had been scant. She'd received a 911 call from the forest, but the cell reception kept cutting out so she had trouble deciphering the message. A group of teenagers had been attacked. There were injuries. No, they didn't know who—*or what*, she had emphasized—had attacked them. She added that the caller sounded stoned and he wouldn't tell her why they had been in the forest.

"You're an EMT, right?" Donny asked Hank.

"Yes, sir."

"Agent O'Dell?"

"No."

"But you know the basics?"

"Very basics. I'm a little rusty."

"Let's do a quick check."

Donny tipped his flashlight back at himself.

"I'm State Patrolman Donny Fergussen. We're here to help. You're not in trouble. If you're hurt, call out. If someone's hurt next to you, call out for them."

Silence. Even the moans went quiet.

An owl hooted. Branches creaked in the breeze.

Finally a voice, a girl's, thin and high-pitched, yelled, "Over here."

Another voice, a male from the opposite side of the darkness. "I'm hurt pretty bad."

Then another girl's voice, on the verge of tears. "I think he's dead. He's not moving. Oh my God, he's not breathing."

Donny looked to Hank, the only EMT. The ranger simply said, "I'll take that one." He shot his flashlight in the direction and followed the beam.

Donny pointed the opposite way to indicate that he'd take the "hurt pretty bad" male. That left Maggie with only her pen-size Maglite to check the girl. She avoided shining it in their faces, scanning for anyone down and not moving. Two girls huddled together under a tree. Maggie tried to get a take on the area while making her way to them. She walked slowly, acutely aware of not disturbing what could be a crime scene.

Hank had led them down through the forest but on the other side of this clearing Maggie could see the rolling hills of pasture separated from the forest by a barbed-wire fence. And close by there had to be a river—she could hear water.

Her penlight picked up something fluttering in the branches, hanging down from a pine tree about ten feet away. She needed to check on the girls first. Maggie swept the light across the path with slow swipes. Every time the beam brushed close, the girls jerked as if the thin razor of light had sliced them.

"Are you two okay?"

They stared at her with glassy eyes. One finally nodded. The other girl lifted her arm to Maggie and said, "He bit me."

Maggie bent down a couple of feet in front of them so she

could get a better look without startling them again. She traced over the girl's arm with the penlight, making the girl jump back.

"I won't hurt you. I just want to see your arm." Still that blank stare. "I'm Maggie. What's your name?"

"Amanda," the girl with the bite mark said and batted the hair out of her face.

Both of the girls were in shock but other than the bite mark Maggie couldn't see any blood. The other girl's eyes stared, still wide and unblinking, at something above and beyond Maggie's head. She turned to track what it was. The dark object hanging from the tree swayed back and forth.

Maggie stood, flicked the penlight up, and pointed as she moved closer. It looked like a dark piece of cloth pierced on the branch. She was almost directly underneath it when she realized it was an owl, hanging upside down.

A dead owl.

Startled, Maggie took a quick step aside and tripped over a log. She lost her balance and fell, hitting the ground hard and dropping her light.

"Agent O'Dell?" She heard Donny call out. "You okay?"

Maggie fumbled in the pine needles, trying to get back up while her hands searched for her penlight. It was still on, about three feet away. She reached for it just as she noticed what it was that she had tripped over.

The beam of light shined directly into the wide-open eyes of a boy who appeared to be dead.

Then he blinked.

SIX

Wesley Stotter knew a back way to the forest. The sandy road became impassable after a little rain but with any luck he'd be out of there by the time those thunderheads arrived.

The grass was almost taller than the Stottermobile. Even the grass growing in the middle of the tire tracks scraped the bottom of his car. The sand sent him sashaying if he went too fast. Yet he pressed down the accelerator. No way could he climb it on foot. Once upon a time he wouldn't have hesitated. He didn't mind growing older until he realized one more physical limitation.

Grasses gave way to trees. Back here were oaks instead of ponderosa pine. The leaves had started changing, some had already fallen. The road wound in such tight turns it was impossible to see what was around the next corner. Branches hung low enough to scratch the car's roof rack. The trees had been planted in straight rows years ago but brush filled in the rows and in the moonlight shadows seemed to spread and devour any openings.

Just a little ways more and he would get to the clearing. A couple more bends to climb around. Then it would be a short hike down to where he believed the radio dispatcher had sent emergency personnel.

He goosed the accelerator a little more, fishtailing in the sand before turning up the next curve. Stotter thought he saw movement to his right between the trees. He slowed and craned his neck to get a better look out the passenger window.

Someone was running. Someone or something.

The front of its face bulged, the back looked hunched. The head swiveled and it looked at Stotter with glowing red eyes.

Then it was gone before Stotter had a chance to decide whether he had really seen anything at all.

He sped up, winding around the trees when a flash of light blinded him.

Stotter slammed on the brakes and held his arms up in front of his face to protect his eyes. The light swept back and forth over the hood. The engine coughed and died. The headlights went dark. He kept one arm up while he fumbled for the keys. Found them and twisted. No response.

The light flashed off. Then came back, piercing him.

A burning sensation raced through his body. His stomach, his lungs, his heart felt like they were on fire. The pain was unbearable, a flame sweeping through his veins. He thought his chest would explode.

And then it stopped.

It took him a minute to unclench his body, to breathe, to open his eyes. That's when he realized the light was gone, too. Only darkness surrounded the Roadmaster. Darkness and silence.

He tried to look out the windows but his vision had blurred. The light had blinded his eyes. He wouldn't be able to see a man—or an alien—if he was standing in front of him at the hood of the car.

Stotter grabbed for the key in the ignition and turned it again.

Nothing.

Usually there was enough battery juice left for the dome light. Whatever that beam of light was, it had knocked out the entire electrical system of his vehicle.

He crawled frantically around, locking all the doors. He climbed over the backseat to retrieve his duffel bag, yanked it open, and started pulling out item after item until he found it.

He wrapped shaking arthritic fingers around the handle of a Colt .45.

SEVEN

———

"I'm not going to hurt you," Maggie told the boy.

His eyes darted back and forth like a wild animal captured.

"Try not to move," she said when she saw the barbed wire wrapped around his body. But he hadn't even attempted to move and she wondered if he couldn't, either from fear or pain. Like the girls, he was definitely in shock.

She swept her light as discreetly as possible, scanning the length of his body. She had to force herself not to wince when she saw the sharp barbs stuck tight into his arms, his chest ... dear God, even his neck. It looked as if someone had rolled the wire around his body, cinching it tight, piercing him deep with every barb. Was it possible he had run into a fence and accidentally wrapped it around himself?

"Ibba ... I ... so hot," he stuttered.

Maggie crawled over and sat back on her haunches. For the first time she saw blood. *So much blood.* She felt it now, slick on her hands and her jeans where she had fallen.

In her ten years as an FBI agent, Maggie had seen cruel and brutal wounds, bloody dismembered bodies, organs left in containers, and only once had she gotten physically ill. But she felt nauseated now. It wasn't the sight of blood still pouring from a live body but rather her inability to stop it.

She thought she had compartmentalized the memories, but suddenly the images flooded her brain of a long-ago killer making her watch. It wasn't the splatters of blood or the victims' screams that haunted her nightmares as much as the sense of complete and utter helplessness. And that's exactly what she was feeling now.

She considered calling Donny but she was afraid to even raise her voice. She was hesitant to move, because she didn't want to startle the boy any more than he already was.

Dark pools of blood covered the leaves and pine needles beneath him. His shirt was wet and rusty with it, and yet the overwhelming smell Maggie noticed was not of blood but of singed hair and burned flesh.

She examined the wire again. She couldn't see a single strand that didn't have barbs. It wasn't the plain electric wires that Donny had pointed out to her earlier.

She leaned in close enough to see that the neck wound had congealed blood around the razor-sharp barbs buried in the flesh. That was good. It wasn't gushing blood, which most likely meant it had not hit the jugular. But his neck muscles bulged against the restraint and a blue vein pulsed against bright red skin.

"Holy crap!" Donny whispered from behind her and Maggie felt a sigh of relief.

The boy's eyes didn't look up at the new voice. They stayed on Maggie's. Hard and tight on her. That was good, too. She had become a focal point for him. Maybe not so good. She had no clue what to do as his focal point.

"I'm not sure if he's still bleeding," she said without breaking eye contact and surprised to hear her voice remarkably calm and steady. "He's definitely in shock."

"Can we move him like this or can we snip him loose?"

Maggie wanted to say, *Aren't you supposed to know? I only know what to do with dead people.*

Instead she took a deep breath and tried to access her internal databank. She had been stabbed several years ago, in a dark, wet tunnel, miles away from help. Another memory, carefully tucked away in yet another compartment of her mind. What she did remember was that she had lost a lot of blood, and she wouldn't have, had the killer left the knife inside her, instead of yanking it back out.

"I think we might start the bleeding again if we pull the barbs out. And I'm not sure he'll be able to stand the pain."

"Holy crap," Donny muttered again.

Maggie continued to watch the boy's eyes, trying to determine if he understood what they were saying. If he did, he gave no indication. His eyes never left Maggie's. She didn't think she had seen him blink since that first time when she stumbled over him.

"Can you understand me?" she asked the boy, slowing

down the question and emphasizing each word. "Blink twice for yes."

Nothing. Just the same glassy, wide-eyed stare.

Then his eyelids closed and popped back open. Closed again and the effort alone looked so painful they stayed closed longer before popping open again.

Maggie's heart thumped hard, relief mixed with a new anxiety. He was conscious and he was in pain.

"I'm Maggie," she said finally. "I'm going to help you."

"Dawdawdaw ... " He babbled, only this time the frustration seemed to drain him. The muscles in his face and neck were tight, his jaw clenched.

Maggie noticed that nothing else moved. His fingers didn't flex. His legs—though twisted into a knot beneath him—did not budge. No part of him attempted to fight or stretch or even press against the barbed-wire restraints.

She scanned one more time, looking for anything that resembled electric wire and checking for burn marks. None, that she could see. Yet the smell of singed hair and burned flesh and the apparent paralysis all seemed to support her suspicions. The boy wasn't only in shock. He had also suffered an electrical shock.

EIGHT

Colonel Benjamin Platt ordered a cheeseburger, ignoring the raised eyebrow and disapproving look from the diner's most senior waitress. To test just how far he could push her, he asked for mustard and extra onions. The waitress, named Rita, had known Platt since he was a med student at William and Mary and pulled all-nighters slinging back lukewarm coffee, hunched over his textbooks.

Back then his attempt at flirting would sometimes win him a piece of stale pie. On a good night the pie came with a scoop of ice cream. Platt couldn't remember when they both had given up all pretense of Rita being his Mrs. Robinson. Instead, she became a sort of mother hen who watched over his heartburn and kept his arteries from clogging.

"Visiting in the middle of the week?" Rita asked as she

poured coffee into the mug without looking, keeping her eyes on his, trying to detect his emotional state. Weird thing was, she could. And what still fascinated him most was that she knew exactly when to stop pouring, right when the scalding-hot coffee reached within an inch of the mug's lip.

"I'm meeting someone," he said. These days he didn't get back to the diner very often except when visiting his parents, who were retired.

She raised an eyebrow.

"No, not that kind of someone." He grinned.

"I would hope not with those extra onions."

Then she turned around and left him, and he swore she added a bit more swing to her hips leaving than she had when she approached.

He smiled again. She could still make him feel like that awkward college boy. Didn't help matters that tonight he wore blue jeans, a faded gray William and Mary sweatshirt, and leather moccasins with no socks. He ran his fingers over his short hair realizing the wind had left it spiked. Just as he glanced at his reflection in the window he saw Roger Bix getting out of a rented Ford Escort. Platt didn't know the man well, but he knew enough to guess Bix wasn't happy about driving a compact anything.

In the glare of the diner's neon sign Bix's shock of unruly red hair looked bright orange, suddenly reminding Platt of the comic-book character Archie. Only Bix was the cocky version, unaware that his paunch hung over his belt. Evidently he thought himself inconspicuous despite the pointed-toe cowboy boots and Atlanta Braves jacket. He looked nothing like a cowboy or an athlete.

Platt waved at him as soon as Bix came in the door. He watched the man scrutinize the surroundings with pursed lips, emphasizing his disapproval. Bix had asked to meet somewhere discreet and totally away from D.C. politicos. Close to Norfolk, where Bix said he had spent the day, and two hours outside the capital, Phil's Diner met the criteria, despite it not being up to Bix's personal standards.

"William and Mary?" Bix said in place of a greeting, pointing at Platt's sweatshirt and letting his slow Southern drawl elongate his sarcastic disgust as he slid into the booth. It seemed there was no pleasing the man tonight. "I took you for a tough guy. Big Ten. Like Notre Dame, maybe. Certainly not William and Mary."

"Notre Dame's not part of the Big Ten. It's a free agent."

Bix shrugged, lifted his hands palms up as if to say college sports was not his thing.

Platt had met Bix several years ago at a conference on infectious diseases. Both were young for their titles, Platt as the director of USAMRIID (pronounced U-SAM-Rid—United States Army Medical Research Institute of Infectious Diseases) at Fort Detrick and Bix as CDC's (Centers for Disease Control) chief of Outbreak Response and Surveillance Team in Atlanta. A year ago they worked together on an outbreak of Ebola, a case that pitted both men against their superiors. The fact that they had retained their positions spoke volumes. That neither man celebrated his victory by making the talk-show circuit or in any way acted like a celebrity revealed a dedication to integrity that couldn't be quantified by a job title. It was, perhaps, the only thing these two very different men had in common.

Rita appeared at their booth again.

"Just coffee," Bix said without even looking up.

"Anything else?"

"Just coffee," he repeated, now with an air of dismissal.

Rita slapped a mug down in front of him and started pouring. Soon Bix realized Rita was staring at him instead of where she was pouring. Platt watched Bix's eyes dart between Rita's and the mug. He was sitting up and preparing for an overflow. Rita lifted the pot without a drip. A sigh escaped from Bix.

"Sure you don't want a slice of peach pie?"

This time Bix glanced up at her and without hesitation said, "That sounds great."

Platt smiled. Rita must have witnessed Bix's entrance, sensed his disapproval, and set things straight the way no one else could. Leveled the playing field in a matter of seconds.

It seemed like a good time to ask, "Why did you call me, Roger?"

Platt waited for the CDC chief to spill one, then two more packets of sugar into his coffee, taking his time, to regain his cocky, self-assured composure. When he finished he planted both elbows on the table, gathered the mug in his hands, and sipped.

There was no hint of levity in his voice when he leaned in and said to Platt, "I called you because I need someone I can trust. I need someone I know can keep his mouth shut."

NINE

Maggie didn't think it possible, but the floodlights made the forest scene even eerier. Stark shadows appeared where none had existed in the darkness. The fallen pine needles and dried leaves came alive. Animals that had been otherwise invisible suddenly became alert, threatened by the light and skittering away. Hank had mentioned something about cougars and bobcats, and Maggie could swear she saw one stalking them from the ridge up above.

Maggie watched as Hank and one of the paramedics gently lifted the boy wrapped in barbed wire onto a stretcher made from a tarp. Rather than carry him up the trail, they had cut the fence that separated the pasture from the forest. They'd take him over the dunes in the back of an ATV to deliver him to a rescue unit waiting on the other side. It was the closest they were able to get a rescue vehicle and they could barely see the halo of the headlights.

Maggie walked with them through the narrow paths of tree trunks, pretending to help carry a corner. She knew the two men could do so easily but she couldn't break the connection with the boy. Earlier, as soon as she started to trail out of his line of vision his head started pivoting around, frantically searching for her. But the paramedic had given him an injection to relax and sedate him and now the boy finally closed his eyes. So she escorted them to where the cattails grew taller than her, to where the ATV idled. One short climb over the sand dune and she knew he'd be safe.

She hurried back and started helping Donny prepare the next of the wounded when she saw a man appear at the top of the dune. Backlit by the headlights behind him, he looked larger than life.

Maggie glanced at Donny who had noticed, too.

"The sheriff?" she asked.

"Probably."

Within seconds another silhouette appeared on top of the hill. Then another. Two more. And still another.

"They know this is a crime scene, right?"

When Donny didn't answer she glanced back at him. He looked like a deer caught in the headlights.

She counted six men. One started down the hill toward them.

"We have to limit how many people come inside the perimeter," Maggie said. "You told me most of the injuries weren't life-threatening, right?"

"That's right. The rescue crew knows we're bringing them

out to their unit. They'll set up a triage area on the other side of that sand dune."

"Then who are these guys?"

The others started following the first.

"Donny?"

"Could be the mayor. City councilmen. Maybe parents. We have two dead teenagers and five injured. They'll want to see if it's their own kids."

"You can't let them come tromping onto a crime scene."

"Nothing I can do about it."

"Excuse me?"

"This isn't my jurisdiction."

"It's not theirs, either."

Seconds ticked off. The men continued single file down the sandy trail, the same path that the ATV had just taken. The men were almost to the cattails. Their heads bobbed in the shadows of the floodlights: one with a cowboy hat, two with baseball caps, the others bareheaded.

Maggie stood up. Donny stayed on his haunches. She shot him a look, hoping to mobilize him. Instead, he stared at the approaching men, accepting the inevitable, this giant of a man silenced, almost cowed.

Then she heard him whisper, "It *is* federal property."

"So it's Hank's jurisdiction?"

She saw him shake his head.

"FBI trumps Forest Service."

Maggie's pulse raced. He was right. She wasn't sure why it hadn't occurred to her. She was the only federal investigator present at a crime scene on federal property. Crap! Officially, that made it her jurisdiction.

She didn't take time to figure it out. Instead, she marched to meet the entourage that arrived at the fringe of their perimeter, almost to the halo created by the floodlights.

"Gentlemen, this is as far as I can allow you."

"Just who the hell are you?"

She opened her jacket, pulling it wide enough for them to glimpse her holstered weapon while she pulled out her badge.

"I'm the sheriff of Thomas County," a short but solid man said as he elbowed his way to stand before her.

"And I'm the county attorney," said the man who glanced at her badge but batted away her hand like her credentials didn't matter. "I handle all the death investigations around here."

"Sheriff, I hope you'll give us a hand," she said while purposely looking at the county attorney. "But the rest of you need to turn around. The forest is federal property." She hoped that she sounded convincing. "This is a federal crime scene. Right now we need to keep access limited. We're trying to bring out the injured while preserving the evidence."

"This is ridiculous," one of the men said.

"How many injured?" the sheriff asked as he stepped closer. "Darlene's radio call never said."

"If these other gentlemen will leave I can fill you in, Sheriff."

"Wait. I think my son is here. I just need to know if he's okay."

"Frank, tell this woman I handle all the death investigations for three counties."

"Gentlemen, please," Maggie raised her voice. "If you'll return to the area over the hill we can continue. We should be able to have some information for you in the next hour."

"This is absolutely crazy. You don't have the authority to tell us what to do."

One of the men grabbed Maggie's shoulder to push her aside.

"These are our kids. We have every right—"

He stopped so suddenly another man bumped into him. They all stared at the Smith and Wesson now aimed at the man's face.

"Lady, you cannot be serious." But he didn't move.

Even the sheriff stood to the side and made no attempt to argue.

The others took several steps backward. Maggie could see beads of sweat on the county attorney's forehead.

"Sheriff," Maggie said, "would you please inform these gentlemen that I don't have the time to make federal arrests right now, but I certainly will do that if it's necessary."

The only sound was the generator, a steady hum up on the ridge, muffled by the trees. A fork of lightning flashed far over the clearing, followed by a distant rumble. A reminder that time was running out.

"I'll let you guys know what's going on," the sheriff said,

and he edged closer to Maggie still keeping a yard between them.

Finally the men turned to leave, casting glances over their shoulders while mumbling to one another. Even the county attorney grudgingly left, after kicking at the ground like a toddler shaking off a tantrum.

When they were past the cattails Maggie said to the sheriff, "I'm Maggie O'Dell."

She holstered her weapon still watching the men, only looking at the sheriff when he said, "I'm Frank Skylar. What the hell's the FBI doing out here?"

"Believe it or not, I just happened to be in the neighborhood." She held back adding "unfortunately." She started leading him back to the crime scene when she added, "I'll need you to call the coroner. See if you can get him here before those thunderstorms make it."

"Well, that's a bit of a problem."

She stopped to look back at him, disappointed that she was still going to have him working against her. "And why is that?"

"You just sent away the coroner."

"One of those men was the coroner? Why didn't he say so?"

"Actually he did. Oliver Cushman is our county attorney. By state law the county attorney is the coroner as well."

It was Maggie's turn to say, "You cannot be serious."

TEN

"I just spent three days in Norfolk," Bix told Platt after chewing two forkfuls of peach pie.

"I'm guessing not at Virginia Beach on vacation."

"Forty-two students at Geneva High School were throwing up their guts after eating lunch in the school cafeteria."

"Food contamination?"

Bix didn't respond.

"Unfortunately it happens more often than we realize." Platt's second bite of cheeseburger didn't taste as good as his first. It certainly did nothing to Bix's appetite. For a guy who wanted "just coffee," he worked his way through the slice of pie like he hadn't eaten all day.

"What was it?" Platt asked when Bix didn't immediately offer an answer. "E. coli? Salmonella?"

The CDC chief put his fork down, grabbed his mug, and slurped coffee.

"Don't know."

"Too early to tell?"

"No. I don't know. I've tested for all six major strains of E. coli and three different strains of salmonella. I haven't found it yet."

Platt stared at him, waiting for Bix to stop looking around the diner as if suddenly he didn't want to talk. Bacteria could be tricky. Oftentimes you found only what you tested for. It wasn't as if you put a sample under the microscope and the various germs lit up in different neon colors. Platt knew there were more than two thousand species of salmonella alone. Most of those existed in animals and humans without causing damage. Some were serious pathogens that could cause a wide range of illnesses and infections from gastroenteritis to typhoid fever.

"Are you saying it might be something we're not used to seeing?" Platt asked.

"Could be a mutated version. I just don't know."

Platt watched the CDC chief fidget with his silverware.

"Was it accidental or intentional?"

"You know some people say our nation's food supply is an accident of epidemic proportions just waiting to happen. We have an administration that's declared child obesity a matter of national security and they want all vending machines out of schools. They want McDonald's to quit enticing kids with toys in Happy Meals. They call Cheerios on the carpet for claiming their cereal reduces cholesterol when Cheerios is not federally approved"—he shot quote marks in the air—"to make such claims. And in the meantime, we have a national food supply that is more vulnerable than ever to accidents, contamination, and tampering. The feds' answer? They need more regulations and yet they don't, won't, and can't inspect what they already have authority over. They're shutting down egg suppliers for a salmonella outbreak but forty-eight hours before that salmonella outbreak, a USDA inspector reported the supplier 'good to go.'"

He shoved the silverware away and pushed back against the vinyl booth. All the while Platt sat quietly, allowing him his rant.

Platt was a soldier. He didn't have the luxury of publicly voicing his political views like Bix, who, despite being a government employee, was still a civilian. That didn't mean that Platt didn't agree with Bix, at least with some of what he said. But it was late. Platt had driven almost two hours to the diner. He had the same drive back waiting for him. He didn't owe Bix any favors. They were even as of Platt's last count.

"What's going on, Roger?"

Bix, finished with the pie, put his elbows back on the table, intertwined his hands, making a steeple of index fingers.

"It's obviously a food-borne illness. Obviously some sort of contamination that took place. All of them ate lunch that day in the cafeteria and within hours they displayed typical symptoms of food poisoning: nausea followed by vomiting, abdominal cramps followed by diarrhea, then fever. That's the first day. I wish they would have called me then.

"The second day, some began passing blood and complained of light-headedness. The third day, several experienced extreme pain. Some hallucinations. There were two seizures."

"When did they call you?"

"This morning. Day four."

Platt only now realized he had shoved aside the plate with his half-eaten hamburger. Under the table his hands balled up into fists. It couldn't be happening again. It wasn't possible. Less than two months ago in Pensacola, Florida, dozens of soldiers who had returned from Iraq and Afghanistan had gotten ill—several fatally—after surgeries to repair or replace their injured limbs. The symptoms had been similar. It ended up being a tissue contamination that no one could have suspected or predicted. Realizing another massive contamination could be happening again, only now at a high school, sent a wave of nausea through Platt.

Bix continued. "Most food-borne illnesses hit those with compromised or weak immune systems—the elderly or little kids. But these are teenagers—their immune systems not yet fully developed but they're not high risk. Whatever this is hits quicker, faster, and harder than anything I've ever encountered."

"Any deaths?" Platt almost didn't want to know the answer.

"No. It's early, but I don't think there will be because, for the most part, these kids are all fairly healthy. That's not to say there won't be long-term effects for some of them. We've got almost a dozen hospitalized and I still haven't been able to find the source of the contamination. I've personally ripped apart the kitchen. Found a few questionable lapses in cleanliness but nothing that warrants this degree of illness."

"What about a kitchen worker?"

He shrugged. "Possible, but we interviewed and tested all of them. No one was sick. Could one of them have contaminated what they served because they went to the bathroom and didn't wash their hands, didn't glove up? I can't say for sure, but this was so severe I'm thinking it had to be a food item that was already contaminated. For it to work this quickly I'm thinking the food had to have an established bacteria settled and waiting."

"Did you find anything in the leftovers?"

"No leftovers. Remember, day four. Everything's already in the trash. Dumpster already hauled off." He held his hands up hopelessly. "I do have the list of what they ate and the suppliers. I could probably spend dozens of hours tracking down whether the contamination happened at the processing plant or at the distribution warehouse or even in the school kitchen. And these schools get stuff from all over the place, not just one center. It's crazy, is what it is."

"This can't be the first time it's happened."

"CDC hears about it only when kids are hospitalized or if there are deaths. Haven't had any reports in months. But schools are notoriously slow about reporting to us. And kids get sick. A lot."

"Waiting until there's forty-two at one time seems inappropriate. What are you finding in the victims?"

"I told you what we're not finding—none of the usual strains. My lab guys back in Atlanta are still searching. It might be salmonella but a mutated strain. Do you remember the spinach recall in 2006? Two hundred and five cases. Twenty-six states. One hundred and two hospitalized. Five deaths. Only five, thank God. That was E. coli 0157:H7, a particularly virulent strain.

"I worked that case. We started by checking all the wrong things. It was E. coli so we were pulling victims' refrigerators and trash cans apart looking for hamburgers, anything with ground beef. Several victims kept telling us, 'No, we don't eat red meat, we're very health conscious.' Spinach was one of the last things we even thought to look at. The victims were healthy but the strain was brutal.

"This reminds me of that case and I don't like it." He tapped his fingers against his lips. "I'm afraid this is going to be something like salmonella on steroids."

"Any chance it's intentional?"

Bix sat back again, the vinyl creaking beneath him. He started to rub his eyes then crossed his arms instead, and Platt figured he had just watched Bix shut down. He was surprised when the CDC chief said, "Yeah, I do. I can't tell you why, but I do suspect it might be deliberate."

"Have you told that to the USDA?"

"I called the department responsible for the school lunch program and they referred me to the new undersecretary of the Food Safety and Inspection Service. All I could get was some lackey in her office who told me that the undersecretary would get back to me after she gets my report and is able to do an assessment. Then she referred me back to the department that I originally called. I hate that runaround crap. And FSIS has a brand-new undersecretary, Irene Baldwin. I don't know her but I already don't trust her. She was the CEO of some huge food corporation. To me it seems a little like inviting the fox in to watch the henhouse."

"Okay, then how about the FBI? Aren't they supposed to be in charge of ... what do they call it, agroterrorism? If this is intentional it would fall under their jurisdiction."

"Right. In partnership with FSIS, FDA, and DHS. But yeah, FBI leads it. They put me in touch with Assistant Director Raymond Kunze. Actually I asked for Margaret O'Dell. I remembered she was the one who helped you crack that Ebola case last year. But I was told she's out of town on assignment. Someplace out west in Oklahoma or Idaho."

"Colorado."

"Yeah, that's right. Kunze is giving me R. J. Tully. He was on the Ebola case, too, but I heard he got suspended. Not sure I like getting second string."

"Tully's good. That case was personal for him. You'd be lucky to get him on this."

Bix nodded.

"I'm not sure why you called me, though. You've got the

FBI. You have some of the best scientists in the country back in Atlanta. If you want me to be a part of some task force, of course, I'll help. But I'm not sure what I bring to the equation."

"Your presence brings the one thing I hope I don't need."

"What might that be?"

"The United States Army."

ELEVEN

After the last of the survivors was removed from the scene Maggie wasn't sure how to proceed.

"I'll radio for Olly Cushman to come on in," Sheriff Skylar told her.

"No, wait. Does the county attorney have medical training?"

"Medical training? Probably as much as you or me."

"I spent three years in premed."

He stared at her. Then finally said, "I'm sure he's taken the same death investigation workshop I did."

"A crime scene like this one is going to require someone with more training than a weeklong workshop."

"Actually, it's a day."

"Excuse me?"

"It's pretty comprehensive," Donny offered, then he

quickly looked away, rubbing at his jaw but it was too late. Maggie had already seen his disapproval.

"You can't examine these bodies out here anyway. We need to bag 'em up, get 'em to a proper facility. Maybe North Platte." Skylar was addressing Donny now as if the two of them would make the decision. "Got to get them out of here before those clouds burst open and wash away any evidence."

"That's exactly why we need to get someone here now," Maggie told him. "I think it's important to examine them at the scene, especially with it being outside. It won't matter how many photos we take. Has Cushman ever investigated a death?"

"Of course he has," the sheriff said. "Beginning of summer. We pulled a woman's body from the Middle Loup. That was a mess."

"Homicide?"

"Accident."

"I thought someone saw her jump from the Highway 83 bridge," Donny said.

"It was ruled an accident."

"What about homicides?"

"We haven't had a homicide in Thomas County as far back as I can remember."

"What about the State Patrol?" Maggie looked to Donny. "You must have someone who serves as a medical examiner."

"We do in Scottsbluff."

He had picked her up in Scottsbluff. From what Maggie remembered of the drive it seemed like an eternity and that was in daylight. She looked over her shoulder.

"We need someone now. There has to be someone closer. Someone in law enforcement with a medical background?"

"There is one person. Just outside of North Platte. She's retired now. Lucy Coy."

"No, not that crazy old Indian woman." The sheriff tucked his thumbs in his belt, looking defiant.

"Lucy follows procedure," Donny said. "We've never had a complaint."

"Of course not. Anybody criticize, she'd probably put a curse on 'em."

Maggie watched Donny's jaw clench. She turned her back to the sheriff and asked Donny, "She has a medical background?"

"I don't think she's a certified MD, but she worked on death investigations with the State Patrol for years. Long before I joined. She taught several of our best investigators. Our course is a week long."

"She probably taught them black magic, too."

"She taught me, Frank."

The sheriff held up his hands in surrender, shaking his head and smiling like he didn't mean anything but indicating that he wasn't really apologizing, either.

"How far away?" Maggie asked.

"Hell, I think her place is just south of here."

"Call her."

"It'd be better to take these kids in and let them get properly examined," the sheriff protested.

"Call her," Maggie repeated.

Donny pulled out his cell phone, checked for reception, and slipped it back in his pocket as he tugged his two-way radio off his belt.

"We could have a downpour at any minute," Skylar still protested. "Everything will be washed away while you wait for Lucy Coy. And then just watch, she'll be collecting spirit dust and lightning bugs. We'll be here till dawn."

This time Maggie pinned him down with a glare that made the man take a step back. Maybe he remembered this was the same woman who earlier pulled her gun on half the county elders.

"I'm still hoping that you'll choose to be a productive part of this investigation, Sheriff." She stopped there when she wanted to ask him to leave, but personal experience had taught her that cooperation from the local law enforcement was vital to winning a community's support. This sheriff could be her greatest asset or her worst liability.

Hank and one of his men returned.

"Hank, do you have some unused brown paper bags?" she asked.

"Yep. Up in the gift shop."

"How about more tarps or rain pouches? Especially anything unused. And rope or twine?"

"I think we can find some."

"We're going to divide this area up into five sections," Maggie explained, "and each of us will work a grid. That's if you're staying, Sheriff?"

They stared at the sheriff. He released a sigh then nodded, just as Donny called out, "Lucy's on her way."

TWELVE

Lucy Coy made her way down to the crime scene as Maggie heard the first drops of rain begin to hit the forest's upper canopy. There was absolutely nothing about the woman that would have prompted Maggie to use or even think the words "old" or "crazy."

She wore hiking boots, blue jeans, a white shirt with the untucked tails sticking out from underneath her rain jacket. Tall and thin, Coy carried herself like a dancer with an elegant but unassuming confidence. Adding to her mystique, there were featherlike wisps of silver in her dark hair that was clipped short. It stuck up in places and would have made anyone else look as if she had just gotten out of bed. On Lucy Coy it looked stylish.

Under the brash floodlights the woman's face showed no distinctive lines, just smooth skin over high cheekbones. Her dark eyes focused on Maggie as introductions were made. The woman was sizing up the FBI agent who had summoned her from her warm, dry home, but with no hint of annoyance. Instead, Lucy Coy looked eager to understand exactly what was expected of her and get right to it.

If anything Maggie could understand the sheriff's awe of Lucy. She seemed out of place with these men, but at the same time she fit in comfortably with these surroundings, almost at home in the middle of the forest. She didn't appear to even notice the rain.

The men from the other side of the hill had brought and left at the perimeter the items Maggie had requested: digital camera, latex gloves, paper bags, markers, and several plastic coolers. Maggie had insisted on unused and sealed tarps to prevent introducing debris to the crime scene. Those were now strung from trees and hung above areas deemed important and waiting for closer inspection or possible casting.

The impact of what had happened to these teenagers was sinking in as each of the injured made their way to the triage area. The boy wrapped in barbed wire had sustained the severest injuries from what Maggie could tell, but that was only if they didn't count the two left behind who waited for Lucy Coy.

Maggie noticed Lucy's rich voice had a tone of reverence. She spoke in perfect rhythm with the breeze and the night birds, offering few words and listening intently.

"We've already taken all the photos we need," Maggie told her. "I thought it was important for someone with a medical background to see the bodies as they were found, before they're moved."

Maggie followed Lucy, who followed Donny. The sheriff lagged well behind as if still pronouncing his annoyance. Yet he wouldn't dare miss this, either.

When the rain had finally come it did so with little fanfare. A rumble of thunder periodically quaked through the trees and sometimes the sky above the canopy would brighten with a soft glow of lightning. But the violent electricity that had forked through the clouds earlier had seeped out somewhere on the horizon. Maggie was grateful and recognized the pitter-patter of the soft rain as a blessing compared to what she had expected. Even the cicadas and crickets agreed and had begun competing with the low hum of the gas generator left up the steep incline, its sound muted by the brush and easily forgotten except for the tentacles of orange extension cords that trailed down the slope.

As they passed under the dead owl still suspended from the branch, Lucy stopped. She stepped closer until she was directly underneath the bird.

"The wings are singed," Lucy said.

Then she bent down to examine the ground beneath the bird. Several orange stakes marked where Maggie had stumbled over the boy wrapped in barbed wire.

"One of the injured was found here," Maggie explained.

Lucy nodded as she swirled a finger in the sand between two areas stained with blood.

Maggie saw the sheriff glare at Donny. Out of the corner of her eye she could see him mouthing, "See, I told you so."

As if that wasn't enough, he spun his index finger at his temple to emphasize that Lucy Coy was, indeed, crazy.

As she stood up Lucy stopped to examine one of the lower branches.

"There's some kind of a thread here," she pointed out. "It's tangled but doesn't look weathered. Can we bag this?"

Donny nodded.

"And the owl. Can we bag it, also?"

Lucy walked around the upside-down bird to look into the creature's eyes. Ignoring the sheriff's reaction to her she added, "Plains Indians believed owls carried the souls of the departed."

"Is that why you want us to take it, because you think it might have captured their souls?" the sheriff asked, trying to keep a straight face.

Maggie was finding it difficult to control her anger at Skylar, and yet at the same time she hoped she hadn't made a mistake asking this woman to join the investigation—a woman whose opinion could be influenced by her ancestors' spirit world, a world that Maggie believed carried no weight in a criminal investigation; a world Maggie had little patience, interest, or respect for.

Lucy Coy, however, calmly went on to explain: "I believe whatever happened to these teenagers also hap- pened to this owl. The way its talons are still gripping the branch"—she pointed to the bird's feet—"along with the singed feathers tells me there's a good possibility this owl was electrocuted."

"Electrocuted?" Donny asked.

"That's ridiculous," the sheriff muttered.

But Maggie's heart skipped a beat. That was exactly what she thought had happened to the boy wrapped in barbed wire and to the two dead victims.

THIRTEEN

VIRGINIA

Platt noticed the car following him soon after he pulled out of the diner's parking lot. At first he thought maybe Bix had forgotten to tell him something and Platt knew the paranoid CDC chief would rather run him down than risk a cell-phone call being traced. But the vehicle following him, five car lengths back, was definitely not Bix's compact rental car. The double headlights sat up as high as Platt's Land Rover.

He took the ramp onto the interstate, goosing the accelerator. The double headlights followed. He switched lanes, crossing over two and watched in the rearview mirror. The double headlights followed, keeping a car in between. Traffic raced around them but the car stayed with Platt. He drove a few miles then crossed back to the right and at the last second swerved to take the first exit. Not so discreetly, now, his tail followed, provoking a horn blare from another vehicle that had to slam on its brakes.

Platt turned into a gas station and pulled up next to a credit-card-only pump. He didn't get out. He waited, ready to floor it if the vehicle followed. It'd be impossible to pretend here, especially after pulling up to one of the pumps. But the double headlights, which he now saw belonged to a black Suburban with tinted windows, didn't even slow down as it passed the station.

Platt sat back, released a sigh. Ran a hand over his face. Relaxed his jaw. Okay, so Bix's paranoia was contagious.

He topped off the Land Rover's gas tank, though he didn't need it to get back home. Then he took several more minutes to wash his windshield, the whole time watching every single vehicle that pulled into the station as well as those passing by on the access road.

Back on the road Platt stayed off the interstate and wound his way through side streets where he could see if he picked up another tail. The amount of traffic surprised him for this time of night, but still, he believed he would notice a black Suburban with tinted windows. Finally deciding it was safe, he backtracked to his parents' house.

They would be up, watching the late-night shows. They'd have Digger between them and all three would have a bowl of ice cream. They doted on the dog like he was one of their grandchildren. Platt's mom would try to talk him into staying overnight, but he'd convince her that Digger would keep him company on the two-hour drive back to D.C. She'd pretend to pout but give him a peck on the cheek and his dad would tell him to call when he got home.

Platt parked and before going in took a few minutes to check his voice, text, and email messages. There were several but none from the one person he was hoping to hear from—Maggie. He knew her plane had landed safely in Denver without any delays. He checked the flight number online to make sure.

He slouched back into the leather seat and shook his head. He had been doing just fine before Maggie O'Dell came along. He had finally found contentment, burying himself in his work, coming home and sitting with Digger on the back porch. He tried not to spend too much time indulging in memories of his daughter, Ali, but Digger was a constant reminder.

In the beginning it was difficult to even have the dog around, but quickly Digger became Platt's shadow, his buddy. He knew the dog missed Ali as much as he did. They had been inseparable or as Ali always said, they were "bestest friends." Now Platt was grateful for the dog's company and for reminding him of the best memories of Ali and not those dark weeks, months, years that followed her death.

Caring about Maggie was a luxury he hadn't allowed himself since Ali's death. Moments like this he questioned the wisdom of it. Being with Maggie, just talking to her—hell, just hearing her voice—made him feel like a college kid again. It was exhilarating. But not hearing from her could make him feel equally miserable. He hated the roller-coaster ride.

So what the hell was wrong with him? He wasn't a kid. He was a colonel, a medical doctor in the United States Army. He was logical and practical and thrived on structure and discipline. He made decisions, solved problems. He went into war zones and hot zones. He had performed surgeries on soldiers while bombs rattled around them. He had treated victims with Ebola working from a tent outside of Sierra Leone. At only thirty-two years old he had seen and done incredible things. Yet nothing compared to the feeling of Maggie sitting on the sofa with him, sockless feet in his lap, while they spent a rare evening watching classic movies or an even rarer Saturday afternoon watching college football.

He looked down at his smartphone again. No new messages in the last five minutes. He pushed Contacts and keyed down to Maggie's number. He clicked on Text Messages and tapped in MISS YOU. XXOO BEN. Then he paused before hitting Send.

Too much?

He tapped Backspace and erased XXOO BEN.

Hesitated again. Tapped Backspace and erased MISS YOU.

Flipping the phone shut, he said out loud to himself, "Coward."

Just as he reached for the SUV's door handle he saw it.

The black Suburban, its headlights off, was stopped at the corner. The vehicle's occupant must have thought it was safe to pull this close, must have thought Platt had already exited his vehicle and gone inside. The Suburban stayed there for only a few seconds longer, just enough time for whoever was driving it to take note of the address. Then it rolled through the intersection. Platt watched it go a full block before putting on its headlights.

Great. Platt had taken some goons to the front door of his parents' home.

He got out of the Land Rover and went around to the backseat to grab a duffel bag. It looked like he'd be spending the night after all.

FOURTEEN

NEBRASKA NATIONAL FOREST

The rain became a downpour just as they carried the last body bag over the hill. The wet grass and sand made the climb treacherous. Maggie nearly fell and she wasn't even carrying a body bag. It was the last compromise she had relinquished to Donny—she let the men carry the bodies. To argue at this point would only be annoying, especially since she was totally and completely exhausted.

She had even given in and allowed the men waiting on the other side of the sand dune to enter the perimeter and help carry out equipment they had used to keep the paper evidence bags from getting soaked. Of course, that was only after Maggie sealed and tagged each bag herself.

The sheriff agreed to lock everything up safe and sound. They'd sort through what they had and decide in the morning where to send the important pieces. Maggie realized there wasn't much of anything to explain what could have caused the teens' injuries. Only one Taser was found in the pine needles. Although it had been fired, the probes were no longer attached to any target and not even close to the two dead boys.

Right now it was time to get out of the rain, find some warmth, and get some rest before morning brought another barrage of tasks. Yet Donny, Lucy, and Maggie stood in the rain as if mesmerized by the red taillights that bounced along the wet, glistening two-track path, now worn wider by more vehicles than it had seen in years.

Donny switched on his flashlight just long enough to glance at his watch. Flicked it off. They continued standing in the rain. Without the hum of the generator or car engines, the song of cicadas swelled around them.

"They must not mind the rain," she said.

Neither Donny nor Lucy responded, but they seemed to understand what she was talking about.

Finally Donny said, "It's after two. I'm not sure what to do with you."

It took almost a full minute before Maggie realized he was talking about her. Originally she had planned to drive back to Denver after a quick examination of several cattle-mutilation sites. She had a room reserved at the hotel where the conference was being held. She was scheduled to teach her first class of the weekend early Saturday morning. She could have saved herself some time by flying directly into Scottsbluff if she didn't mind getting on a twin prop. She did, however, mind very much.

"She'll come home with me," Lucy Coy said matter-of-factly.

Donny nodded as if neither of them expected Maggie to have a say in the decision.

And oddly enough, Maggie didn't protest. When they moved to leave, Maggie simply followed. She pulled her leather satchel from Donny's vehicle. Her suitcase was still in the trunk of her rental car, left in the parking lot of a Scottsbluff mall.

"I'll have someone get your rental in the morning," he told her. "I'll call our field office. Make sure the car and all your stuff is secured for the night."

She wanted to tell him not to bother. There was nothing of value in the suitcase that couldn't be replaced. Instead, she simply thanked him and got inside Lucy's vehicle. Maggie took note of the wood paneling and soft leather seats and smiled. Finally something Maggie might have expected from the woman. Lucy drove a Jeep Grand Cherokee but one loaded with luxury and elegance. There was something comforting about that. Perhaps Maggie had not entirely lost her edge in profiling people.

As they bumped over the rough trail, Maggie stole a glance at the woman's regal profile in the blue-tinted dashboard lights. Maggie was mentally and physically worn out. Her rain-soaked clothes stuck to her skin. Despite a good rubbing from the towel Lucy had offered, Maggie's hair dripped into her eyes. The blast from the heater only emphasized the chill that had invaded her body. Never had Maggie trusted a stranger, let alone gone home with one she had met only hours before. Yet there was an undeniable comfort being in the presence of this woman.

Maggie shifted in her seat, pulling up her leg to tuck underneath herself. She thought about Platt and had the sudden urge to hear his voice. She checked the dashboard clock: 2:16. Just after three in the morning his time. She didn't want to wake him. Instead, she sat back and closed her eyes.

FIFTEEN

NORTH PLATTE, NEBRASKA

Dawson Hayes opened his eyes. Plastic tubes shot out of his arms and nose. He startled and gasped and somewhere a machine hissed and gurgled. He'd been dreaming about birds with scalding white eyes perched over him in the tops of the forest's highest pine trees.

He searched for the woman's eyes—the soft brown—that held him above the pain and promised not to drop him. Where was she?

His eyelids fluttered despite his panic. He tried to keep them open. A shadow over him said, "I think he's waking up."

Two blinks means "yes."

But Dawson couldn't blink. He couldn't hold his eyelids open.

Half a blink was all he could manage but it was enough to see the shadow insert a needle into one of the tubes.

"No, no ... not," he stuttered, his throat suddenly raw and dry. Something was stuck down it. He couldn't swallow. It hurt to breathe. Unfamiliar hums and beeps assaulted his ears.

Then he saw the fiery red eyes across the dimly lit room. The creature had followed him. How was it possible?

He struggled and strained but couldn't move. Something clamped him down. He opened his mouth to scream but the contraption in his throat choked him. He tried to open his eyes beyond the half shutters that blurred his vision.

Then he felt it, warm liquid sliding into his veins. But it was pleasant and soothing. Whatever the shadow had injected into the tubes had started to invade his insides. He felt it seeping into his brain and he imagined it racing along his arteries, replacing cold blood with soothing liquid warmth that made his mind fuzzy and his heart stop exploding.

Another shadow stood over him. This one leaned down and he caught the scent of pine needles and river mud mixed with sweat. Dawson felt hot breath on his ear as he heard the shadow whisper, "You're gonna wish you hadn't survived."

SIXTEEN

"The sheriff's a man who means well," Lucy Coy said.

She handed Maggie a tray that held a bowl of steaming homemade chicken noodle soup, half a sandwich with layers of deli slices on a plate garnished with fresh strawberries and blueberries, and a mug of spiced tea. It took discipline for Maggie to wait for her host to get settled.

"He'll make sure those teenagers are properly taken care of," Lucy continued. "Even the dead."

They sat on the screened-in porch off the second-floor loft of Lucy's contemporary A-frame house that looked like something out of *Architectural Digest*. The porch looked into treetops and over Lucy's backyard. When the moon broke through the clouds Maggie could see rolling hills dotted with pine trees, the landscape unbroken for miles by fences or another homestead.

The rain had turned to mist. Once in a while it came in on the breeze. But Lucy had turned on an electric fireplace in the corner and the outdoor room became a cozy retreat. Behind the sliding glass door was the loft with a queen-size bed waiting for Maggie. She felt too tired to sleep and when Lucy offered a bite before bed, Maggie gratefully accepted. She hadn't eaten since morning, a banana and a Diet Pepsi on the flight from D.C. to Denver. She'd forgotten about crossing back and forth over three time zones. Her head and stomach were still set on eastern time. No wonder it felt like days.

Besides, for months now Maggie had been unable to shake a bad case of insomnia. As an FBI agent she had learned to compartmentalize her mind, carefully stowing away the awful images she had seen and all the brutal experiences she had survived. Lately those compartments had started to spring leaks and it usually happened after dark.

Nightmares played a loop in her mind, reliving the experiences, sometimes in freeze-frame, sometimes in high-definition. She hadn't discovered a remedy. Nothing worked. Not warm milk or alcohol, exercise or quiet. The only thing that had ever worked—but only once—was Benjamin Platt's strong, soothing fingers working the tension from her shoulders and back. Although it was only a massage and hadn't led to anything more, just the memory of it still made her flush.

Two of Lucy's dogs, a gangly retriever mix and a three-legged boxer, came in and curled up at their mistress's feet. Earlier, a pack had met the Jeep and escorted it down the long driveway to the house. Lucy had explained that people kept leaving their castaways at the edge of her property, knowing she'd take them in and thereby assuaging their guilt by not turning them in to the pound for a sure death sentence. When the headlights swept the side of an out-building Maggie had seen a couple more snouts peeking out of the small doors crafted into the shed.

A black German shepherd nudged Maggie's elbow for a handout.

"Jake," Lucy scolded in her low, gentle voice and the shepherd lay down by Maggie. "Usually he's not this friendly. He showed up about a month ago, but he comes and goes as he pleases. He'll be gone for days at a time."

"Maybe he has another home somewhere."

"I don't think so. He comes back scraped up and starving. Hank thought he saw him in the forest one night. Worries me because they've also reported seeing a cougar. No, I think ole Jake just hasn't decided if he wants to call this home." Almost on cue the dog laid his head on Maggie's foot.

"I have a white Lab," she said. "Harvey. He sorted of ended up on my doorstep, too."

"So you rescued him."

"I like to think we rescued each other."

Lucy smiled, a first since they'd met, then she wrapped long fingers around her mug of tea and sat back in the wicker chair.

"What do you think happened out there tonight?"

Maggie asked. "It couldn't have been just a game of Taser tag, could it?"

"I've never seen Tasers do what we saw tonight," Lucy said, then seemed to consider it as she sipped. "Things aren't always what they seem. For years ranchers used barbed wire for fencing. Cattle respected the boundary because it hurt to cross it. Intruders respected it because the barbs look vicious and dangerous."

Maggie listened patiently, remembering the woman's explanation for bagging the owl. Perhaps this was how she answered classroom questions, with proverbs and folk tales.

"Now some ranchers use the electric fencing. Unlike the barbed wire, the electric wire looks quite harmless. You can't tell if it's hot, if it's dangerous, until it's too late."

Maggie quietly sipped her tea. Reached a hand down and petted Jake who released a heavy sigh before flopping onto his side to expose his belly. Without looking over at Lucy, Maggie said, "So what the hell does any of that mean?"

To Maggie's surprise Lucy laughed, hard and long. She had to wipe her eyes before attempting an answer. And when she finally did, she prefaced it with "I think you and I are going to get along just fine.

"It simply means don't dismiss something that appears ordinary. Outsiders come here and they tend to see a simpler life, an uncomplicated people. But human nature is human nature. People out here are capable of the same things as people in cities. You might think it's easier to hide the

87

mistakes, the evil—if you will—in the city, but sometimes it's just as easy to hide things in plain sight."

Lucy set her mug down and reached into her jacket pocket, pulling out what looked like bib lettuce in a Ziploc bag. She held on to it, fingering it carefully.

"I think this is *Salvia divinorum*. They call it the sage of seers. The non-*divinorum* is the salvia you find in gardens and flower beds. This is a psychoactive species of mint. It grows mostly in Mexico and some southwestern states. The Mazatec people believed it had spiritual and healing properties. You dry it and smoke it, or you wad it up when it's still green"—she held up the bag—"and chew it. They say its hallucinatory properties are more potent than LSD. It's the newest rave for teenagers."

She fingered the bag and then looked directly at Maggie when she said, "I found this under one of the dead boys when I was examining him."

"And you put it in your pocket?"

"Sheriff Skylar is a man who means well. Possession, distribution, and sale of salvia is illegal in more than a dozen states. Including Nebraska. There was a young woman whose body was found in the river several months ago. Some say she was tripping on salvia. Thought she could fly and jumped from the Highway 83 bridge. That bridge is a hundred and fifty feet above the water.

"There were friends with her at the time. No arrests were made. There was no mention of drug use. It was said to be an accident. Sometimes it can be devastating for grieving parents to learn bad things about their dead child. I thought it was important that this didn't accidentally get lost or misplaced because of good intentions."

Lucy set the plastic bag on the side table between them, relinquishing it, handing it over to Maggie.

"I'll understand if you no longer want me to participate in this investigation."

Maggie left the bag on the table, sipped her tea, and considered what Lucy had done. In most cases it could be viewed as obstructing a federal investigation. Perhaps even tampering with evidence and certainly not following the chain of command. What was it that her old boss and mentor, Kyle Cunningham, would say? "Rules were made for the head to judge when the heart got in the way."

Finally Maggie looked over at the woman and said, "I think you and I are going to get along just fine."

FRIDAY, OCTOBER 9

SEVENTEEN

Mary Ellen Wychulis waited outside her new boss's office. The undersecretary of Food Safety and Inspection Services hated tardy employees but obviously didn't mind keeping them waiting. Mary Ellen crossed her legs and let her foot tap out her annoyance.

She was missing her son's first official playdate. Her husband had emailed three photos—mostly blurs of babies surrounded by too many toys—but they were enough to make her ache. She had only been back at work three weeks and already she wished she had taken some extra time.

It didn't help matters that she returned to a new boss; her old one, promoted up the ranks, had been kind enough to make sure her job was secure before he left. These days that was no small feat. And so she was grateful even if her new boss was obsessive-compulsive, an outsider who Mary Ellen believed was an obvious political pick.

Mary Ellen felt like she had spent the last three weeks teaching her the nuts and bolts of the job. But she held her tongue even when she realized her husband was, most likely, right. Had she not been pregnant, her previous boss would have recommended Mary Ellen for his old position. She didn't like to admit that such bias still ran rampant in the federal government, especially at the upper levels. Had she been a man with the same qualifications, age, marital status, and even a new baby, she would, no doubt, be the new undersecretary.

The door to the office opened so suddenly that Mary Ellen startled. A man in a military uniform marched out then turned back.

"Keep me posted," he said.

Mary Ellen could see that her boss, Irene Baldwin, had followed him to the door. The officer looked familiar but Mary Ellen couldn't put a name to the face, although she realized he resembled too many military elite—thick-chested with steel-gray hair, a rubber-stamped scowl, and lifeless eyes.

She watched the man march all the way down the hall before it hit her. General Lorimer was the chairman of the Joint Chiefs of Staff. Off the top of her head she couldn't think of a single project her boss was supposed to be working on with the Department of Defense. She wondered what brought him here.

"Wychulis. Good, you're on time. Enter," Irene Baldwin said with a wave of her hand then darted back into her office before her last guest had even reached the elevator.

Baldwin had changed the office so remarkably from its previous occupant that each time Mary Ellen walked in she had to remind herself she worked for the government, not a Fortune 500 company. But it was also a reminder that Baldwin not only *had* worked for a Fortune 500 company but *had* run one.

Where framed black-and-white photos of agricultural history had hung on the walls, there were now canvases in vibrant-colored oils with abstract images that on closer inspection could depict stalks of grain or bird's-eye views of a forest. The new wall decorations looked like they belonged in a contemporary art museum instead of the office of an undersecretary in the Department of Agriculture.

"Sit," Baldwin told Mary Ellen.

Her one- or two-word commands reminded Mary Ellen of dog obedience school.

Baldwin continued to stand behind her desk and pull file folders from a neat stack piled on the polished corner. The only other things on the desk were three pens and a legal pad.

"I have questions," she said, sorting through the contents of a file folder.

Mary Ellen sat on the edge of her chair. Of course, she had questions. Every morning she had questions and she expected Mary Ellen to save her precious time by providing the answers. Mary Ellen kept her back ramrod straight, her feet flat on the floor, preparing for whatever Baldwin wanted.

"I have a request to continue"—Baldwin paused to put on a pair of reading glasses—"something called a mobile slaughter unit in Fort Collins, Colorado. What exactly is that?"

"It's part of the 'Know your farmer, know your food' initiative. The unit travels from site to site and provides services to small regional producers at a host farm."

"Services?"

"Yes."

"Slaughter services."

"That's correct." Mary Ellen refrained from any more details. One thing she had learned about Baldwin—and learned the hard way—was that the woman enjoyed making a game of what she believed were the agency's "absurdities" or "foibles." Despite Mary Ellen's recent absence she had almost five years invested at the USDA and a loyalty to public service. She didn't appreciate the sarcasm even if some of it was justified. Of course any agency had problems.

Baldwin came from the private sector. She had worked her way up the ranks of a large food corporation, ultimately becoming responsible for developing the research facility which was known worldwide for its cutting-edge labs. It was no secret that she was hired to bridge the communication gap between the Food Safety and Inspection Service and the private processors and distributors who provided the nation's food supply. Her experience would give credibility to an agency that had the reputation of beating up on those same processors and distributors that it was supposed to work closely with, not just regulate to assure the safety of the nation's food supply.

"Second question." Baldwin pushed at the glasses that tended to slide to the end of her nose. "Why do I have a citizen's petition from"—she paused again as she flipped pages—"a Wesley Stotter, who says these mobile slaughter units are, quote, being used for unethical and secretive government experiments, unquote?"

"I'm not familiar with that petition."

"No?" Baldwin slid the file to Mary Ellen's side of the desk. "Please read it. Stotter is a syndicated talk-radio guy. Looks like he has a rather significant audience, though a somewhat strange mix of antigovernment and UFO fanatics. Could be nothing. Could be a media headache waiting to explode into a migraine. Last question."

Her curt, brisk style had Mary Ellen's head spinning and stomach turning the first several days.

The woman pulled another file from the stack.

"What in the world is a 'spent hen' and why is there a pending review waiting for my confirmation?"

"Spent hens are old egg-laying birds, past their productivity. Most commercial buyers like fast-food restaurants or processed-food companies won't buy them. The hens spend most of their lives caged while laying eggs so their bones tend to be brittle and can splinter."

"Doesn't sound like much of a review. Brittle bones would definitely be a food-safety issue. If no one wants to buy them, why is there a review?"

"Well, actually for the last decade the USDA has bought them. Millions of pounds, in fact."

"What on earth for?"

Mary Ellen fidgeted with the pages in her lap. There was nothing else in the folder except the document asking for confirmation from Baldwin to continue the review. Mary Ellen wanted to kick whoever had put this on her boss's desk in the first place. She didn't want to hear her boss's sarcasm and judgment, even if she agreed.

"Wychulis, I have only the request. Please enlighten me. Why in the world did the USDA buy millions of pounds of brittle-boned chickens?"

"For the National School Lunch Program."

EIGHTEEN

———

NEBRASKA

Maggie had slept. Hard enough that she needed to remember where she was. The scent of brewed coffee and freshly baked bread wafted up to the loft, but when she looked over the side rail she didn't see Lucy in the kitchen.

The woman had loaned Maggie an oversized T-shirt to sleep in. It looked new and had blocks of brightly colored train cars with a logo that read RAILFEST 1999. She found her clothes, which had been soaked and stained with blood and debris, now freshly laundered and stacked neatly on an upholstered bench by the stairs. Even her shoes had been cleaned, the mud scraped off and the leather polished. She wondered if Lucy had slept at all.

Maggie opened the sliding glass door to the porch and stepped out into the morning sunlight. Blue skies—not a patch of white cloud—stretched over miles of sandhills, the yellow and burnt-orange grasses waving so that the hills looked like they were actually moving.

Directly below—what Maggie had not been able to see last night—were a patio and landscaped garden with brick-paved pathways between berms of flowers. Colorful birdhouses hung from trees. A small fountain made of watering cans trickled a stream down onto rocks. Maggie could hear wind chimes and smell pine. And in the middle of this paradise was Lucy's tall thin figure, arms stretched above her head, the wide sleeves of her shirt and the slow, graceful movements of her arms looking like wings of a bird.

Sheriff Skylar had mentioned Lucy's Indian heritage and Maggie wondered if this was, perhaps, part of a silent tribal dance. Lucy saw her, completed the circle her arms had started, and then shouted up, "You're welcome to join me for a little yoga before breakfast."

Maggie was glad she was far enough away that Lucy couldn't see her embarrassment. Yoga. Of course, it was yoga. What was wrong with her? She was as bad as Skylar.

"No, thanks. Do I have time for a short run instead?"

"That's fine. Help yourself to whatever you can find in the closet and the bottom drawer of the bureau."

Maggie found shorts and a sweatshirt. Thankfully Lucy wore baggie workout clothes. Her shoes were a bit long but Maggie fixed them by putting on two pairs of socks. In minutes she made her way out the long driveway with Jake, the black shepherd, following along.

Last night she hadn't noticed that the road to Lucy's place was hard-packed sand with only patches of gravel mostly in the middle. The rain had left crevices that ran like veins and crumbled the edges. Maggie stayed close to the center, not risking sliding into the rain-filled ditch.

At first the shepherd seemed confused by her behavior, on alert, looking for whatever danger had made her run. But he kept pace and soon stopped looking over his shoulder. It reminded her of jogs with Harvey. She liked having the company.

They hadn't been at it for long when the dog's ears pitched and he started herding Maggie to the side of the road, bumping her leg once and then a second time when she ignored him. The pickup came roaring over the hill from behind them. The tires sent a spray of sand at Maggie and Jake as it swerved to avoid hitting them. The dog crouched to his belly. The brakes screeched, spitting more sand and gravel. Taillights flared. The truck jolted to a stop about ten yards ahead of them.

Jake was back on his feet, his nose nudging Maggie's hand, wanting her to follow him back to the house.

The engine idled then the driver shifted into reverse and slowly backed up. The window opened and a man poked his head out. He was young, mid-twenties with a sunburn and ball cap pulled low so that all Maggie could see were his mirrored sunglasses and a bushy mustache.

"Everything all right, ma'am?"

"Just out for a run."

"A run?" His head swiveled around as if he were looking for someone else to explain.

"I'm jogging," she said, noticing that her mouth and eyes were lined with sand.

He stared at her. Then finally said, "Oh sure. Okay. Just thought I'd better check."

He shifted gears and slowly drove off. She could see him watching her in the rearview mirror and realized that it was curiosity more than remorse that had slowed his speed.

When she and Jake got back to the house, Lucy had the table already set for breakfast and had added the scent of bacon to the kitchen.

"You forgot to mention what an oddity I might be, out running in the road."

Lucy didn't look up from the counter where she slathered butter on bread, but there was a glimpse of a smile when she said, "I think you and I were meant to be oddities no matter where we are or what we do."

NINETEEN

NORTH PLATTE, NEBRASKA

Light blinded Dawson. He jerked awake to find sunlight streaming through the blinds of his hospital-room window.

Sunlight. No laser beams or fireworks.

His dad sat up in the chair beside the bed and rubbed at the stubble on his face and the sleep in his eyes. Dawson wondered how long his father had been there. Had he seen the creature? Dawson frantically searched around the room.

"You're in North Platte," his father said, thinking he must not recognize his surroundings. "At the hospital. You got banged up pretty good but you're gonna be okay."

His dad looked tired. But he always looked tired. He worked ten-hour shifts at the meat-processing plant. Sometimes he pulled a double shift when one of the other security guards called in sick. He even worked part-time on his days off, couriering packages. He didn't used to put in this many hours when he was a state patrolman. But he left that job years ago. Dawson didn't know the details and he didn't really care. It happened right about the time his mom left them. In fact he'd barely noticed that one day his dad was getting ready for work and holstering a Taser instead of a Smith and Wesson.

They didn't even have dinner together anymore, let alone talk to each other. Except for when his dad felt it was necessary to tell Dawson how disappointed he was in him. Dawson figured this would be one of those times, especially if his dad had spent the night sleeping in that vinyl chair.

"What happened?" Dawson asked, hoping to preempt the lecture.

"You don't remember?"

He stared at his father trying to decide whether he would even believe him. A creature with red eyes shooting electrical sparks out of its arms? His father mistook the confused look to be a loss of memory.

"The doctor said you might have short-term amnesia. You got an electric shock from something. He's thinking it was strong enough to throw you into a barbed-wire fence. You ended up with it wrapped all around your body. You don't remember anything?"

Dawson didn't respond. His father was standing now. Not a tall man but from the bed Dawson felt as if the man towered over him. Then his dad did something totally unexpected. He put his hand on Dawson's shoulder and for a brief moment Dawson thought he saw sadness in his eyes.

"You're really lucky, kid. A couple of your friends are dead."

It didn't register. How could any of them be dead? They were just screwing around. Having some fun. Who was dead? Dawson didn't get a chance to ask.

"Hey, Mr. H," a voice called from the doorway and suddenly Dawson's dad was smiling. The sadness was gone and so was his hand from Dawson's shoulder.

"Johnny. How's that throwing arm?"

"Sore, but I guess I can't complain."

Dawson thought Johnny B looked better than after a football game. What he couldn't believe was how excited his dad looked, as if a celebrity had walked in, but then Johnny B was the closest thing there was to one in town.

"Is it okay for me to talk to Dawson?"

"Sure. I need to get home and change for work. I'll leave you boys. Dawson, I'll be back tonight as soon as I get off, okay?"

Johnny waited for Dawson's dad to leave and even then, took a place beside the bed where he could watch the door.

"What did you tell him?" he asked.

"Excuse me?"

"What did you tell your dad happened last night?"

"Nothing. I didn't tell him anything."

"Did you tell him about the camera?"

"No."

"What about the Sally-D?"

"Of course not."

"You know we could be in a whole shitload of trouble if they found out where we got it."

"I didn't tell him."

"They'd drop me from the team. All those scholarship offers will be gone if I end up not playing."

"I didn't say a word."

"I'll never go anywhere." And then under his breath, "That'd make Amanda happy."

Dawson had never seen Johnny like this—more scared than angry.

"None of it was my idea," he said. "I go down, everybody goes down."

"My dad said somebody died."

Johnny stared straight ahead, somewhere over Dawson's head. Then suddenly he gripped Dawson's bandaged arm, digging his fingers into the wounds. Dawson wanted to scream from the pain. He saw fresh blood staining the wrap. He tried to jerk his arm away but Johnny tightened his grip, leaned down until his face was inches from Dawson's, his breath hot and sour.

"Just keep your mouth shut."

TWENTY

———

Julia Racine wished she could stop thinking about how sticky the little girl's hand was. She should be grateful that CariAnne wanted to hold her hand. Truth was, when Julia finally gave in to dating women, she thought that at least she wouldn't have to deal with children. Too often the men she had dated wanted her to be instant stepmom to their weekend kids. Julia knew long ago that she didn't possess that maternal gene. She realized that she never wanted to be a mother long before she even realized her preference for women.

She didn't admit it to anyone, but children grated on her nerves. She didn't have the patience for either their bouts of exuberance or, at the other end of the spectrum, their constant whining. Her new partner had recently suggested—after seeing how uncomfortable Julia seemed to be with her daughter—that perhaps Julia hadn't gotten the chance to be a child herself and so she couldn't relate. To which Julia had muttered, "Thank you very much, Dr. Freud," but at the same time she remembered thinking, "Duh. You think?"

Julia was ten, just a little older than CariAnne, when her mother died. Her father tried to make Julia's life as normal as possible and she absolutely adored Luc Racine for his efforts, but something broke inside Julia the day her mother left. She knew that then, although she didn't understand it. But she had felt it, like fabric that had tugged and stretched then ripped at the seams. It had been a pain, an ache so real, so palpable that as a little girl she truly believed something—her stomach, her intestines, her heart—had surely been torn.

Her father claimed that one day she was climbing trees and the next day she was pulling up a chair to the kitchen sink to wash dishes, trying to do her mother's chores herself.

"It just wasn't natural," Luc would finish off the story. Although these days Alzheimer's prevented him from remembering his own daughter at times, let alone remembering that story or his long-gone wife.

Perhaps Julia's lack of maternal instinct really did come from not having a real childhood. For years she blamed it for her inability to sustain a normal relationship. Only recently had it occurred to her that it might have something to do with playing on the wrong team. So here she was, trying again. Really trying this time. If someone was keeping track she should get mega points for this—picking up Miss Sticky Fingers from school *and* having to wait in the principal's office for approval.

Needing to get the proper approval, even though her partner had filled out all the necessary forms, didn't bother her. As a police detective, Julia appreciated rules that protected kids from perverts. It certainly made Julia's job easier. But there was something about waiting for the principal, no matter what age you were, that was unsettling.

She glanced at the large institutional-size clock on the wall. Must be standard issue. Julia remembered a similar one from her elementary-school days. And she had spent plenty of time outside the principal's office back then. Even as a kid she hadn't had patience. Being too grown-up at age ten—or at age thirty-one—didn't seem to stop her from telling her peers how stupid they were. Except now that she wore a gun they tended to not argue back as often.

A woman came rushing into the outer office. She knocked on the principal's door but didn't wait for an answer before she opened it.

"I counted sixty-three lined up for the nurse," she said, staying in the doorway. "That doesn't count those still in the restrooms."

A voice answered from inside but Julia couldn't make out what was said. The woman's head swiveled around, only now noticing Julia and CariAnne. She stepped inside the office and the door slammed shut.

Julia tugged her hand away from the little girl and quietly got up to glance outside the door. A line of kids snaked around the corner. Some were holding their bellies. Others were leaning against the wall. A few adults manned the line, feeling foreheads and offering whispered reassurances.

"Do you know what's going on?" Julia asked CariAnne.

"A lot of us haven't been feeling good since lunchtime."

"You don't feel good? You didn't say anything?"

"I don't usually have to. Mom just knows."

Julia looked back out the door, thinking they sure had everything under control for all these kids not feeling good. But then all it took was one to start vomiting. The little boy barely made it to the trash can. Watching from the sidelines, Julia thought it looked like dominoes, one kid after another, bending, gagging, retching and the few adults like tops spinning from one end of the hallway to the other.

It was almost funny until Julia heard CariAnne behind her. The little girl was reaching for her hand again, holding her stomach, and pressing against Julia. In seconds she, too, was bent over and spraying Julia's shoes.

TWENTY-ONE

Even without the barbed wire Maggie thought Dawson Hayes still looked fragile in the stark, white hospital bed. She felt an odd connection to him and couldn't shake how his eyes had pleaded with her, depended on her.

This morning his arms were wrapped in blood-stained bandages. An IV tube snaked from the back of his hand to a machine. She and the sheriff were told that a gastro-intestinal tube had been removed from his throat so he might be a bit hoarse. And that they shouldn't push him to talk too much.

The scratches on his face looked raw against his pale skin. The bandage on his neck hid a wound that seeped. But the thing that bothered Maggie most was that the boy still looked scared.

Sheriff Skylar had insisted he direct the interviews with the teenagers. They were kids from his area. He knew many of their parents. They'd feel more comfortable talking to someone they knew rather than a state patrolman or an FBI agent. She agreed, letting him believe that in doing so, he had won a major concession, when in fact, Maggie didn't actually have official approval to proceed as lead investigator.

She had left a message for her boss, Assistant Director Raymond Kunze, but she hadn't heard back from him yet. She already knew what he'd say: "Hand it off to the locals. You have a conference to attend."

The "locals," Maggie had discovered in the meantime, would be either the FBI field office in Omaha, two hundred and eighty miles away, or the Forest Service in Chadron, which was two hundred miles away. Kunze wouldn't comprehend that distance, nor would he care what difference losing the first twenty-four hours could make.

Besides, detouring her to visit the site of a cattle mutilation was, no doubt, only a favor he had been repaying, one of those courtesies that government officials gave each other. Maggie suspected Kunze hadn't intended for her to give any of it more than a cursory look and write the obligatory report that would be his proof of repayment. If he had intended for her to actually create a possible profile of the cattle mutilators, he certainly would have included many more of the details in the file.

Truth was, it didn't matter. Maggie didn't want the case. She'd never been a lead investigator. Her job had always been to assist law enforcement agencies at their request. She was the outside observer, the specialist who could be objective and catch details that might otherwise be missed. She liked being the outsider.

Earlier she'd decided to stay long enough to make sure as many pieces of the investigation—especially the collecting and processing of evidence, including witness accounts—was placed in the hands of officials who could properly take over.

So she didn't argue with Sheriff Skylar.

She didn't like hospitals—who did? She wanted to be back at the crime scene. That's where Donny Fergussen was. At Maggie's request, he was meeting a State Patrol crime-scene unit. They'd go over the area again, widen the perimeter, cast several footprints, and collect any other remaining traces that the tarps hopefully had preserved. She would much rather be out there than with Sheriff Skylar. Witnesses were notoriously inaccurate, and a bunch of teens tripping out on salvia would probably be worthless narrators of what had happened last night in the forest.

But Maggie wanted—no, she needed—to see that Dawson Hayes was okay.

"Dawson, I'm Sheriff Skylar. Your dad used to work with me."

Maggie studied the boy's face, watching for signs of recognition. If he knew the sheriff there was no relief in seeing him. Was he worried about being in trouble?

Skylar didn't wait. He pulled a chair from the corner and placed it beside the bed. As he sat down directly in the boy's line of vision, he threw a thumb over his shoulder and said, "This is Agent O'Dell from the FBI."

Dawson's eyes swung up to hers then darted back. It was enough for Maggie to see his panic was real now.

She remained standing and stayed by the door where she could watch not only Dawson but Skylar as well. When Skylar told her he wanted to conduct the interviews, it was because the teenagers would be "less rattled" with someone they knew. So she was surprised when he began by saying, "We know about the Taser, son," immediately putting the boy on the defensive.

Earlier the sheriff couldn't wait to tell her he had already traced the serial number on the Taser back to Dawson's father who used it for his job as a security guard at a meat-processing plant outside of North Platte. Skylar had explained that the gun was standard issue at the plant and all he had to do was check their database. Possession of the Taser seemed to be Skylar's smoking gun, so to speak, though there was no evidence it had caused any of the injuries.

Maggie would quickly regret not changing the subject.

"Did you shoot any of your friends with the gun, Dawson?"

"No, absolutely not."

"Come on, Dawson. I know it was fired. You might just as well fess up. We're going to find out the truth soon enough."

The boy's eyes looked up at Maggie, to Skylar, then back

to Maggie, staying with her for a beat longer, imploring her as though she might be the more understanding one.

"I shot at ... something," he said.

Instead of leaning in for the explanation, Skylar sat back and shook his head like he had heard this before and didn't have the patience to hear it again.

"So what was it you think you shot at?"

"I'm not sure. I didn't really get a good look. It had red eyes. Maybe a wolf."

Now Skylar jerked forward, surprised.

"A wolf? You sure it wasn't a coyote? Maybe a cougar? Hank said there's a big cat of some sort in the forest. They've had sightings. But wolves? We haven't had wolves in this area since I've been here."

"I don't know. I guess it could have been a coyote or cougar. It was big. And white."

"White?" Skylar sat back and shook his head again. No longer interested. "A white wolf or cougar."

"It pounced at me. I shot at it. I'm pretty sure I hit it."

"There weren't any animal tracks," Skylar told him, his arms crossed over his chest.

The sheriff wore a flannel shirt this morning, a black-and-red plaid that somehow made him appear bigger. Maggie realized the sidearm strapped at his waist probably had something to do with the appearance, too. Last night she hadn't seen any weapon under his jacket.

The boy looked at Maggie again, but she had nothing to offer. There had been plenty of footprints all over the sandy floor of the forest but no animal tracks, at least none the size of a wolf or coyote or cougar. The pine needles could have disguised an animal's presence, but a wounded animal would have certainly left prints.

Then Maggie remembered. The girl named Amanda had been bitten on her arm. Could it have been an animal? What did she say about it? "*He* bit me." Last night Maggie hadn't thought to ask. It seemed a minor issue compared to the girl's shock and the other teens' injuries.

"Dawson, I'm disappointed. I didn't expect you to lie when two of your friends are dead."

"It's true. It was watching from the brush when the fireworks were going off. It had red eyes."

"Fireworks. Right."

Last night, while they were being treated, some of the others had mumbled something about fireworks or a light show. Hank had been within a mile of the teenagers' campsite and hadn't seen any display, nothing close to fireworks or a laser-light show like the teens described. It could have been the salvia.

At some point Maggie would need to fess up about the plastic bag Lucy had found. She was hoping to have it analyzed before handing it over with the other trace evidence. If Skylar had kept the existence of drugs a secret during a previous investigation, she wouldn't risk him doing it again. She certainly didn't expect any of the teenagers to offer up information about the drug.

Perhaps Skylar read her mind.

"What kind of drugs were you tripping on?" he asked.

"Excuse me?"

"You kids might think I'm an old man, but I'm not stupid. I know you weren't in the forest at dusk sitting around drinking soda pop. Not the first time you've been out there either, is it?"

Maggie had to give the man some credit. Sometimes this type of interrogation opened a spigot when the subject felt guilty and just needed an extra push to spew out a confession or give up some vital information. But this would not be one of those moments. Maggie didn't think Dawson Hayes looked guilty. He looked scared.

When the boy met her eyes this time, his eyes stayed on her. She saw the panic soften and give way to a spark of recognition.

"You're the one who found me," he said.

"Yes, that's right."

"You should have just let me die with the others."

TWENTY-TWO

Organized chaos. That's exactly what Benjamin Platt saw when he arrived at Fitzgerald Elementary School. Police officers with whistles guided a line of cars with disheveled parents picking up the last of the children. A group of what looked to be school administrators and teachers were helping paramedics escort children to waiting ambulances. The frenetic energy spilled across the street to bystanders and into the neighborhood where people watched from their front lawns.

As Platt got out of his Land Rover a cable-TV camera crew started setting up. He recognized the well-dressed anchorwoman eyeballing him, trying to decide whether or not he was someone important. By the time he flashed his credentials at the first police officer, Platt could hear the newscaster calling out to him. Too late. He slid his messenger bag higher on his shoulder, strode on without a glance back.

He made it up the steps before another uniformed cop stopped him.

"Essentials only beyond this point, sir," the cop told him.

Before Platt could respond he heard a woman from inside the doorway say, "It's okay. He's been cleared."

Tall, lean, attractive but with a hard edge and a clenched jaw telegraphing *don't mess with me*. Her short blond hair spiked up in places as if she had just come in from the wind, though there wasn't a breeze. She wore street clothes: jeans with a tucked-in knit shirt tight across full breasts and a shoulder holster displaying her Glock nestled close underneath her arm, so that anyone who dared to admire her physique also got an eyeful of the metal, another warning not to mess with her. Her badge hung from her belt but Platt didn't need to look at it. He recognized the District detective.

"Hello, Detective Racine."

"CDC guy's waiting for you. I'll take you to him."

"Thanks. I'd appreciate that."

Not even five feet inside, Platt immediately smelled the sour vomit, splatters of it left on the floor. Otherwise the hallway was eerily quiet. Racine led the way, unfazed by the smell. Platt glanced into the empty classrooms. They rounded one corner and suddenly had to step aside for two men dressed in full SWAT gear.

He waited for them to pass before he asked Racine, "What the hell's going on? I thought this was a food contamination?"

"Mr. CDC called in a domestic terrorism alert. Sixty-three

kids puking up their cookies all in a matter of an hour. Tends to trip an alarm or two."

"Any fatalities?"

"Not that I'm aware of."

"Aren't you homicide?"

"Yes."

Platt stopped mid-stride to look at her.

"I was already here," she said.

"Excuse me?"

"Off duty. I was picking up my partner's kid."

He started walking again. "Picking up your partner's kid, that seems beyond the call of duty," he said, trying to lighten the tone.

"Not my professional partner. My personal partner."

"Oh." He didn't know what to do with that tidbit of information. In the few times he had met her at Maggie's house, he hadn't picked up on the fact that she was gay. He chose to not comment. "Does Bix know you were here when it started?"

"Bix?"

"The CDC guy."

"No. We're here to secure the area. That's all we bring to this party. He doesn't much care what else we have to offer. FBI and Homeland Security have people here."

Platt nodded. Sounded like Bix was getting all his ducks in a row, so to speak. But for a guy who wanted to keep things under wraps, he couldn't be happy with the entourage of news media already setting up.

Earlier when Roger Bix had called Platt he only doled out scraps of information but had been adamant that this school's incident was, in fact, related to the one in Norfolk, Virginia. When Platt asked how exactly he knew they were connected and what new information pointed to that—after all, just last night Bix didn't even know what had caused the contamination in Norfolk—Bix would only say, "I have it on indisputable authority that these two incidents are, indeed, related."

Obviously from the show of force Bix knew much more than he was willing to disclose. Platt wondered how the hell he could help if the man had already decided not to trust him.

"When I finish with Mr. Bix I'd like to talk to you about what you saw," Platt told Detective Racine as they turned another corner. "Would that be possible?"

"Sure. I'm not going anywhere for a few hours." She pointed to a doorway and added, "I'll be out front."

She turned and left him. Even after she disappeared around the corner he could hear her heels echoing down the hall. The only other sound came from beyond the open door, hushed voices giving orders. One of which Platt already recognized.

Two men in dark suits shouldered past Platt on their way out, leaving only three people in the small office. Bix had a cell phone pressed against his ear as he sat behind a desk with a nameplate that proclaimed it as Principal Barbara Stratton's. Ms. Stratton, most likely, was the woman in a navy suit with long silver hair tied back. Platt wasn't surprised to see the third person, Special Agent R. J. Tully.

The tall, lanky FBI agent had been leaning against a corner but stood straight when Platt entered. He offered his hand while Bix only nodded and continued to make demands to some poor soul on the other end of the phone line.

Platt had met Agent Tully on the same case that Bix had referred to last night. It was the same investigation where Platt had met Maggie O'Dell. Almost a year ago a madman had stuffed envelopes with the Ebola virus and sent them to what appeared to be random victims.

Maggie had been exposed and ended up in a USAMRIID isolation ward at Fort Detrick under the care of Platt. The case had taken a personal toll on Tully as well, resulting in his suspension during an internal investigation that eventually cleared and reinstated him. When Platt recommended Agent Tully to Bix last night, he did so knowing that Tully was one of only a handful of people Maggie trusted. For Platt that was justification that he met Bix's criteria.

Platt exchanged greetings with Ms. Stratton then asked her to fill him in. She glanced at Bix as if looking for permission but only momentarily.

"At first I thought it might be some kind of prank. In my thirty-two years I've never seen so many children ill at the same time. It was awful. Absolutely awful. And it happened so suddenly. My secretary noticed a line to the nurse's office and not fifteen minutes later the line had doubled. Then I heard children vomiting in the hallway. Some of them using the trash receptacles. Others holding their bellies and not able to get to the restrooms, which, by this time, were also backed up."

"Did you notice any odd smell prior to the students getting sick?"

"What kind of smell?"

"Anything out of the ordinary."

"We have a school full of children. There's no such thing as ordinary smells."

Platt smiled until he realized she wasn't joking.

"I think Colonel Platt means something like natural gas." Agent Tully stepped in. "Rotten-egg gas, perhaps, or any strong chemical smell."

"Oh, heavens no. Nothing like that. You think a chemical could have caused this?"

Bix snapped his cell phone shut with enough of a clap to draw everyone's attention. He stood up, sending Ms. Stratton's desk chair smashing into the back wall. He ignored the scowl from the principal as he unleashed his outrage at her.

"You didn't tell me one of your cafeteria workers was sick when she reported in this morning."

"What? This is the first I'm hearing about it."

"She's at the front entrance babbling to the police officers that this is all her fault."

"That's not possible! We abide by the highest standards."

"Right. Well, she came back after the evacuation. Appears

she has a guilty conscience. Admitted she wasn't wearing gloves today."

"We require gloves on all our kitchen servers."

"Well, it sounds like her gloves were a bother. She got tired of taking them off to blow her nose."

TWENTY-THREE

NEBRASKA

The girl was lying.

Maggie tamped down her impatience. She was beginning to think these interviews were a waste of time. She glanced at her watch. Maybe the autopsies would reveal more. She leaned against the bedroom wall next to a bookcase topped with stuffed animals belonging to a much younger version of the girl they were now talking to, although her mannerisms seemed to slip into little-girl mode as the questioning progressed.

Sheriff Skylar's kid-glove treatment of Amanda Vicks was in stark contrast to what he'd put Dawson Hayes through. Yes, Dawson had been in possession of a Taser, but there was no evidence, as of yet, to prove any of the teens had been shot with the gun. And Dawson had been severely injured. Amanda only had a bite mark on her forearm that she couldn't seem to explain beyond her declaration at the scene that "He bit me."

Now when Maggie asked, Amanda said she couldn't remember where or when she was bitten. If it had been a wolf or cougar certainly she would have remembered, but Maggie didn't press the matter. They had taken photos of the injury. She'd trust Lucy Coy to determine whether it was animal or human sooner than she'd trust the memory of a girl who had most likely been tripping out on a hallucinogen when the incident happened. And to Maggie, that was further evidence that this interview was probably worthless.

Maggie wondered if Sheriff Skylar knew the girl was lying. Perhaps that was why he was taking a gentler approach and using a different interrogation technique on her. However, earlier he seemed much too polite with Amanda's mother, Cynthia Griffin, and the girl's stepfather, Mike Griffin. On the drive over, Skylar had mentioned to Maggie that Mrs. Griffin's family—the Vicks—owned several businesses in the area, including the meat-processing plant, a ranch, and two area banks. Maggie was sure she must have misunderstood about the banks—no one owned banks anymore, did they?

Skylar pulled up a chair, keeping a safe distance from the bed, unlike the menacing stance he had taken with Dawson. Whatever the sheriff's intention, Maggie remained quiet. After her only question about the bite mark she stayed back out of Skylar's way and out of the trailing vapor of

Amanda's annoying incense. She wanted to keep the girl off center and slightly outside her nice, warm comfort zone.

If it had been up to Maggie she would have questioned Amanda outside of her bedroom, another of Skylar's decisions that she didn't agree with, but not necessarily a bad one. Maggie decided to use it to her advantage. There was such a thing as a witness being too comfortable. Maybe she'd catch Amanda off guard with some of her own interrogation tricks, like simply standing instead of sitting. It made the witness have to keep track of two interrogators even if both weren't asking questions. Being on different levels accentuated the effect. Sometimes the interrogated lost track of his or her story—or lie—needing to watch for a reaction from two people.

It appeared to be working.

The girl's bloodshot eyes flitted from Skylar to Maggie and back to Skylar, trying to stay on the sheriff. She batted at her blond hair, pushing tangles out of her face. It looked as if she hadn't brushed it yet today. She held on to a water bottle and absently took the cap off and screwed it back on, but Maggie noticed her coordination was off. Every few seconds Amanda stopped and gulped a few swallows like each sentence left her mouth dry.

"I know it's not easy to talk about but can you tell us what you saw, Amanda?" Skylar's questions came soft and gentle like he was coaxing a kitten out of a tree.

"It's hard to describe," she started to answer, eyes darting to Maggie. Her hands made the plastic water bottle crackle as she squeezed too hard and tightened the cap, then immediately started unscrewing it again.

"The lights came out of nowhere. We were, like, just sitting and talking. Then there's this flash of light. It was like one of those big strobe flashes on a camera."

She took a sip from the bottle. That was it. She was finished with her story. Maggie wanted to ask how soon had they seen the lights after they chewed on the salvia. She knew Amanda wouldn't be confessing anytime soon to using any drug. Maggie also guessed the salvia wasn't the girl's first experimentation with drugs. Skylar had to see that, didn't he? He'd questioned Dawson about drugs. Certainly he would ask Amanda.

"How about sound?" he said instead. "Did you hear anything unusual?"

"Oh yeah. It was really weird. Sort of like a hum. No, maybe more like a purr."

"You mean a purr like an animal?"

Maggie could see the girl peeking out from behind a strand of hair, looking at Skylar as if waiting for him to give some hint as to the correct answer.

"I don't think so. Then there was this sort of sizzle. You know like when you first throw a hamburger on the grill."

Skylar winced at the comparison. If she wasn't mistaken, Maggie thought the girl seemed pleased by his reaction.

"What made that sound?" Skylar asked. "Did it come

from above? Did it seem like it was coming from the lights?"

This time Maggie had to stop herself from wincing. He was offering too much information. Why was he leading this girl?

Amanda simply shrugged and tried to put the cap back on the bottle. She missed. Looked down and tried again. Maggie noticed the girl's hands were steady. There was no shake or tremble from nervousness. She didn't see any of the signs of fear in Amanda that she had seen in Dawson's eyes. In fact there seemed to be nothing uncomfortable about recounting the incident, and Maggie realized it had nothing to do with her lack of coordination.

"Did you see what happened to your friends?"

This time she looked like she was actually thinking about the event for the first time.

"When the flashes went off, me and Courtney were sitting to one side. I got up and then I sort of pointed at the fireworks. It looks so pretty I can't take my eyes away. I didn't see Trevor and Kyle. Johnny was with us and he was sort of stumbling around because, you know, he's looking up at the lights, too, and we're all oohing and aahing."

Maggie wished she had suggested they record the interview. She lost track of how many times the girl switched from past tense to present and back. Forensic linguistics was about as scientific as criminal profiling, but each had undeniable benefits. To find a probable truth in someone's statement you analyzed not only their choice of words but also the tense. When describing an event from memory most people used past tense. If they switched to present at any time when telling the story, that part was more likely to be a fabrication than the truth. Amanda had switched tenses several times and without pause. She also managed to do so without giving them any details, so that her mingling of fact and fiction didn't much matter.

"She needs to get some rest," Amanda's stepfather said from the doorway, and Maggie wondered how long he had been standing there. She hadn't heard him come up the hallway. "Mandy wasn't even supposed to be there last night."

"That right?"

"She was supposed to be at Courtney's studying. She's been tired a lot lately. Too many demands on her time."

Maggie watched Amanda while the men talked about her as if she wasn't there. She caught the girl rolling her eyes. Both men missed it. Her stepfather seemed a bit too proud that Amanda was so popular that it would exhaust her this early in the school year. He sounded more worried about her overextending herself than about the fact that she had lied about her whereabouts. Either he didn't know about her extracurricular activities outside of school or he didn't want to know.

Griffin's concern evidently was enough for Skylar. He flipped his notebook closed, satisfied to call it quits. When he stood up he saw Maggie still standing by the bookcase. He looked like he had forgotten about her.

"I think we're done here. That is unless Agent O'Dell has any questions for Amanda."

"Just one," Maggie said and she patiently waited for Amanda's eyes to flit back up to her. "Do you usually get high this early in the day?"

TWENTY-FOUR

———

Velma Carter wiped her bloodshot eyes and couldn't look at Platt.

"We were already short two people," Carter explained. "I couldn't call in sick another day." She sunk her chin into her chest and shook her head. "Those poor babies. All my fault. I didn't mean to make them sick."

"But you didn't think about that when you took off your gloves." Roger Bix's rage was brutal. He had been looking for someone to shred and now he believed he had found the culprit.

"Roger," Platt tried to interrupt him.

"We'll need to test you." Bix was unrelenting. "See just what the hell you've been spreading."

The woman started sobbing again. When Detective Racine brought her in the small office, the woman's face was already red and blotchy. Racine hadn't left and no one suggested she do so. She stood quietly aside, shifting her weight from one foot to the other. Platt didn't think she was comfortable with Bix's approach, either.

"What the hell were you thinking," Bix continued and this time Platt stepped in between the two.

"Ms. Carter, I'm Dr. Benjamin Platt." He left out the "colonel." No sense in putting this poor woman more on edge. "We'll need to take a couple of test samples from you. Is that okay?" They'd need both blood and stool samples, but he'd tell her that later.

She pulled a tissue from somewhere up her sleeve and blew her nose. He could hear the rattle inside her chest. But it sounded like typical cold or flu symptoms. Nothing that would give almost seventy children such immediate nausea and diarrhea.

Platt didn't look at Bix. He wanted him to know he was cutting him off, but from the corner of his eye he could see that the man's face was as bright as his orange hair. Platt couldn't help wondering what had Bix wound so tight, much too tight. He was treating this woman like a terrorist with a bomb strapped to her chest. Yet last night when Platt had suggested a kitchen worker might be the culprit, Bix had dismissed the idea.

"I'm going to have someone come and take a few samples. Is that all right with you, Ms. Carter?" Platt waited for the woman to nod.

"Hell, I'll take the samples myself." Bix was at it again.

"No, Mr. Bix," Platt said, leaning into Bix until the man had to look him in the eye. "We'll send someone in." He looked over at Racine. "I saw some paramedics earlier. Are they still here?"

"I'll go check."

"We'll be right back, Ms. Carter. Can I get you anything?"

She shook her head as Platt grabbed Bix by the elbow and escorted him out of the room. He kept walking, pulling Bix along until they were halfway down the hall.

"What the hell is wrong with you?" Platt asked. "Last night you told me this could *not* be a norovirus from improper food handling. You implied it had to already be in the food. Now you unload on that poor woman like she planted the bacteria in every lunch she served. What aren't you telling me?"

"Doesn't it make you a little mad when food handlers are so negligent?"

"So you feel better now after lecturing her? Because we both know that unless she has some highly contagious virus or sprayed contaminated body fluids over seventy kids' meals, she did not cause this."

Bix shoved at Platt's hand, though Platt wasn't even holding on to him anymore. He stood up straight, threw back his shoulders, stretched his neck, and stared at the ceiling. Then he released a sigh and looked at Platt. But still there appeared to be no urgency to explain.

Platt just shook his head. "You're going to tell me later

whether you want to or not. Right now we should start retrieving whatever we can. Before it's gone."

"Except we don't know what we're looking for at this point."

"Yes, we do. Undoubtedly, these kids got sick after having lunch in the cafeteria. So let's go see what we can find of today's meal even if it means scraping it off the hallway floor and the bathroom stalls."

TWENTY-FIVE

NEBRASKA

Maggie needed to get to North Platte for the autopsies, so this next interview would have to be her last of the day. That was if Skylar didn't strangle her before they got there.

"What the hell were you thinking?" The red-faced sheriff had blasted her as soon as they got back to the car.

"The girl's high. Probably marijuana. That's why she has the incense burning. Her eyes are bloodshot and dilated. Her coordination is off. I can't believe you didn't see that."

"She's been through an incredible experience. Of course she's not herself."

"Why didn't you ask her about drugs? You told Dawson Hayes that you knew why they were out in the forest."

"Amanda's not a suspect."

"Neither is Dawson."

"He had a Taser. A Taser that had been fired."

"But we don't have a victim who's been shot with a Taser."

"Not that we know of." Skylar wouldn't relent.

"Look," Maggie said, calming herself and her tone, "next time you decide someone's a suspect, please inform me."

"Next time you decide to insult the daughter of one of our community's most respected business owners, please inform me."

She shook her head and left it alone for the drive to the Boshes'. It was thirty-five minutes away. The kids lived in different towns but all attended the same high school; one high school for the entire county.

The Boshes' two-story Colonial, which sat on a huge lot that backed to the city park, predicted what Maggie could expect from this interview. She didn't need to ask whether Skylar believed this boy was a suspect. Before visiting the Griffins' house the sheriff had already told her that Johnny B had recruiters from five major NCAA teams at the last football game. But he was going to make them all proud by staying in Nebraska and playing for the Huskers.

"Might even start as a freshman quarterback," Skylar had gone on. "He's something to watch. Got an arm on him and man, that boy can scramble. He can get himself out of every kind of mess."

So Maggie would need to either steel herself for another kid-glove interview or make a decision to take over this investigation.

Mrs. Bosh was waiting outside the front door when they got out of the sheriff's SUV. She was an attractive woman with a pinched, worried face. She wore slacks, a white silk blouse, and leather pumps. Perhaps she had taken off work early or she had dressed for her son's interview.

Before they reached the front steps she called out, "He isn't here."

Skylar turned to look at the red Camaro in the driveway but before he could ask, Mrs. Bosh continued, "He was here when I came home for lunch. I just got back a few minutes ago and I can't find him anywhere." She held up a cell phone. "I checked with a couple of his friends. They haven't seen him today."

Maggie realized she hadn't been sympathetic enough. These kids just lost two friends. Here she was arguing with Skylar about whether they should treat them like suspects or witnesses, when all of them—until the evidence said otherwise—were victims.

Mrs. Bosh came down the steps rather than invite them in. She looked over her shoulder as if worried someone would see her.

"I'm worried he may have taken some of my pills."

"What kind of pills?"

Another glance over her shoulder.

"Painkillers. For my back when my car was rear-ended last spring."

"I doubt the boy would take something like that, Mrs. Bosh." Skylar patted her arm.

"What kind of painkillers?" Maggie wanted to know.

She hadn't worked narcotics but had read about teenagers raiding their parents' medicine cabinets for drug parties. If these kids were using salvia and Amanda was high in the middle of the afternoon, there was a good chance they had been experimenting with other things.

"There weren't very many left. I just noticed the empty bottle this morning."

"Mrs. Bosh, do you remember the name of the painkiller," Maggie insisted.

"Yes. It was OxyContin."

Now Maggie was worried. Experimenting with OxyContin could be fatal. It was a time-release medication, but chewing or crushing it caused rapid release and a lethal amount of the drug could flood the system.

"What was Johnny like this morning? Did he seem depressed or upset about last night?"

"Agent O'Dell, Johnny is an athlete," Skylar said before Mrs. Bosh had a chance to answer. "This is a kid who's going to be a number-one recruiting choice." He was giving her the same look he had when they left the Griffins' house.

"He seemed really nervous and sort of jumpy." Mrs. Bosh ignored Skylar and spoke to Maggie. Her eyes kept sweeping up and down the street. "He wasn't himself."

"Did he talk about what happened last night?"

"No. He wouldn't talk about it. And my husband said we shouldn't make him." Then her attention got distracted and she tilted her head and walked to the edge of the sidewalk. "Do you hear that?" she asked.

They listened. Other than a train whistle in the distance,

Maggie heard birds, a wind chime, nothing more. Then suddenly she did hear something. A soft whimpering.

Mrs. Bosh headed around the side of the house, hurrying through a flower bed instead of going around it. Maggie and Skylar followed. At the back of the house a dog laid on its belly, whining.

"Rex, what's wrong?" But Mrs. Bosh didn't go to the dog. Instead she stayed back, standing stock-still.

"Does he belong to you?" Maggie asked.

"The neighbor's. He comes over and Johnny plays ball with him. They've been playing since Johnny was a boy."

Maggie approached the dog carefully. He didn't appear injured. He focused on something under the porch. Maybe a toy had gotten lodged or an animal was trapped underneath. But the dog's whine sounded more urgent than playful.

"There's a crawl space," Mrs. Bosh said. "It goes all the way under the house but we put a board down there so animals couldn't hide."

Maggie pulled the penlight from her jeans pocket and kneeled down, coaxing the dog to move enough for her to take a look underneath the porch.

"Johnny used to crawl all the way under there when he was a little boy. He usually did it when he was in trouble and didn't want to be found."

That's when Maggie noticed a small, torn piece of fabric snagged on a nail.

"What was your son wearing this morning, Mrs. Bosh?"

TWENTY-SIX

Maggie remembered that the reason she had a rental car, now stuck in Scottsbluff, Nebraska, was because she refused to get on a twin-prop airplane. She understood it wasn't an actual fear of flying so much as a fear of being without control, which was often the crux of most fears. If you had control over a situation, there was nothing to fear. That's what Maggie kept telling herself as she crawled through the dirt underneath the floorboards of the Boshes' house, using her elbows to pull forward.

There was, at most, two feet from top to bottom, which kept her on her stomach. Some areas were tighter. Cords and cobwebs hung from the two-by-fours, getting tangled in her hair. A loose nail had already bit into her shoulder, tearing away a piece of skin and fabric just as it probably had with Johnny.

They had tried to shine a high-powered flashlight through the opening but support beams blocked their view.

Mrs. Bosh called to the boy but no one answered. When Maggie suggested one of them go in after him, she swore she could see the color drain completely from Skylar's face. Now, as the smell of mold and dirt filled her nostrils and dust mites floated in the flashlight streams, she questioned her own judgment.

The tightness squeezed around her, support columns scraping against her shoulders. Memories of being trapped seeped into her consciousness. This was not so much a memory as a distinct feeling that suddenly washed over her body. She had to stop, catch her breath. She tried not to panic when that breath filled her lungs with musty particles that threatened to block her intake of air.

It had been several years ago when a killer threw her into an empty chest freezer. She could remember clawing at the inside door, her fingernails broken, the tips of her fingers raw and soon numb. Most times the only overpowering memory was the cold, so deep and unbearable that her mind had shut down. Eventually her body, too, had collapsed from hypothermia.

She closed her eyes for a minute. Told herself to slow down.

Breathe through the mouth. Deep, steady breaths.

She couldn't start hyperventilating or she would be in trouble. She shoved the memory aside. It was cold down here but not freezer cold. This was different. She wasn't trapped. She had control.

She crawled and wiggled her way ahead. As the passage

began to narrow, she started wondering how she would turn around.

Stop thinking about it.

Mrs. Bosh's voice became more and more muffled.

Skylar had set up the high-powered flashlight at the opening under the porch, but the shaft of light couldn't bend around corners or through support columns. At this point all she had was her penlight.

Something skittered on her left. Fur brushed her hand. Maggie jerked and cracked the top of her head against a two-by-four. It was just a mouse, she told herself. Too small for a rat. But she still shivered.

Not a rat. Stop thinking about rats.

She stopped and readjusted, giving her elbows a rest.

"Johnny? It's Agent Maggie O'Dell. Do you remember me? From last night?"

She paused. Listened. Nothing. Except now she thought she heard a voice. Garbled but definitely coming from somewhere in front of her.

"Johnny. We're just worried about you. You're not in any trouble."

Her penlight couldn't show her what was beyond the next support column, this one thicker, the width of two rows of cement blocks. She must be at the center of the house. The sound came from the other side of this column.

She palmed the penlight and held up her fist so that she could see the path ahead of her as she crawled. There was more space here, at least an additional foot higher. The narrow stream of light caught glimpses of objects in the dirt. On closer inspection Maggie recognized discarded toys, a Star Wars action figure, candy wrappers, and crumpled soda cans.

She pulled herself even with the support column and rolled to her side. She realized she could actually sit hunched over. She leaned against the cold cement blocks and took a few seconds to bat the cobwebs out of her face and hair. One swipe with the penlight and she saw him.

He was sitting with his back to her, less than ten feet away, slouched sideways and leaning against another column. She could hear him mumbling.

"Johnny?"

No response.

If he was tripping on OxyContin or more salvia, he might be incoherent.

"Johnny?" She tried calling to him again.

She could move on hands and knees here as long as she stayed low. Still, her back scraped against wires stapled to the floorboards. Her shirt caught on another stray nail. This time she ignored the rip of fabric and kept going. She came up beside him but he didn't acknowledge her presence. She put a hand on his shoulder, trying not to startle him as she dragged herself around.

In the halo from the penlight she saw his eyes and she knew immediately. She could see the earbuds and the dangling cord. The mumblings she had heard came from his iPod, not from Johnny.

They were too late.

TWENTY-SEVEN

Julia Racine had never really understood what Maggie O'Dell saw in Benjamin Platt. He seemed too disciplined, too spit-and-polish, too much of a play-by-the-rules type of guy. Though she did have to admit he had a nice ass.

Of course, she still noticed stuff like that. When it bugged her partner, Rachel, Julia would usually say, "Hey, I'm gay, I'm not dead."

Truthfully, she'd always imagined Maggie going for some-one who was a bit more adventurous, a little unpredictable and passionate. Someone a little more like ... okay, some-one a little more like Julia.

She followed Platt out to the school parking lot after offering to help.

"At least there's no camera crew set up back here," Platt said while his head swiveled around to make sure. "I couldn't believe they beat me to the scene."

Julia actually *could* believe it. The vultures always somehow found their way. Now she was living with one of them. Just a year ago if someone had told her she'd fall for a card-carrying journalist she would have said they were crazy. And maybe she was nuts. For the second time in about an hour she caught herself hoping Rachel hadn't been the one to tip off the vultures.

She followed Platt to the Dumpster in the corner of the lot. It was surrounded by a six-foot wooden fence, closed with a padlock.

Platt slapped at the lock. "How bad are things when we start locking up our garbage?"

"Makes it more difficult to dump dead bodies."

He glanced at her like he hadn't thought about that before. Funny, it was the first thing that popped into Julia's head. Too many times she'd had to help fish some poor victim out of a Dumpster—usually a woman. Men rarely got thrown in with the garbage. In fact, one of the last cases Julia and Maggie had worked on together included a decapitated woman whose head Julia had found in the victim's own kitchen trash bin.

"This is a little messier than you bargained for," Platt said, giving her an easy out.

It made her smile. He definitely had no idea what kind of messes she had been exposed to in the past. But he did have a point. It was Julia's day off. She didn't need to do this. She didn't even need to be here.

Maybe she was simply curious about Benjamin Platt. She

used to have a big-time crush on Maggie but then somewhere along the line they had become friends. The two of them had more in common than either wanted to admit. Both had lost a parent during childhood. Both of them had to fight their way up the ranks of male-dominated careers. They trusted very few people and allowed even fewer in their lives, so friendship was not a term either threw around lightly. Fact was Julia respected the hell out of Maggie and maybe she wanted to see who this guy was that had snagged her attention.

Julia watched as Platt took off his jacket and carefully placed his wallet and cell phone in one of the jacket pockets before folding it and setting it on the concrete. She kept from rolling her eyes as he turned up the cuffs of his shirt in perfect folds that matched on both sides. Then he surprised her and scaled the fence in three moves.

Julia stood back, hands on her hips. Okay, so that was not expected. Maybe he was a bit more adventurous than she gave him credit for. But of course, he was athletic. You'd have to be blind to not notice his lean physique. She just didn't expect him to get his trousers dirty or his polished leather shoes scuffed.

"I can toss some of the bags over," he said.

"No, don't bother."

"Yeah, you're right. They'll break."

She knew without looking that there would barely be room to stand between the fence and the Dumpster. She could hear him shoving open the lid and immediately smelled the garbage.

She took off her jacket and laid it next to his, not folding hers quite as nicely as he had. She decided to keep her shoulder holster on. Then she followed him over the fence, almost as smoothly except for the splinter that ended up in the palm of her left hand. Sharp and deep—it took biting her lower lip to keep her from releasing a string of expletives. She had been trying to watch her mouth around CariAnne, after the little girl kept riding her about her overuse of the "f-word." Nothing like having a nine-year-old lecturing you on manners. After all, Julia could just tell her to fuck off like she would if it was anyone else.

"So what exactly are we looking for?"

She handed Platt a pair of latex gloves. She had grabbed several from the kitchen. Habit. Platt looked surprised to see them but immediately started putting on a pair.

"Anything from today's menu."

"They didn't just leave us some leftovers in the fridge?"

"That'd be too easy." He smiled as he yanked a piece of paper from his back trouser pocket and unfolded it. "They had something called a taquito. Any idea what that is?"

"CariAnne loves those. They're her favorite school cafeteria meal. It's sort of like a burrito but fried."

"Beef or chicken?"

"Either, but she likes the ground beef better. They also have cheese, onion, some kind of sauce. We've tried to duplicate them at home but, according to CariAnne, there's something we keep missing."

"I forgot to ask, is she okay?"

"She puked all over my shoes, but she's resting at home now with her mother who knows when she's sick even without CariAnne having to tell her." Silently Julia told herself to shut up. Why did it bother her that she hadn't automatically seen that the little girl hadn't been feeling well? She couldn't be expected to know that, right?

"I guess that's a special mother talent the rest of us don't have," Platt said, as if reading her mind, but he wasn't joking. Instead, Julia thought he looked ... if she wasn't mistaken, she thought he looked sad.

"Do they make them or are they premade and frozen?" He was back to digging in the garbage.

For a second Julia had forgotten what they were talking about. "I don't know for sure, but I'm thinking they'd have to be premade and frozen. No way they could make hundreds of those by hand in a morning."

Platt looked at the list again. "They also had lettuce salad and oatmeal cookies."

Julia's stomach growled. Platt raised an eyebrow. The rancid smell had not dissipated, nor had the flies.

"Missed lunch," Julia said without apology. Digging through garbage didn't gross her out any more than scraping brains off a wall or watching a medical examiner crunch through a rib cage. When you're hungry, you're hungry. Except today she still couldn't shake the smell of the kids' vomit.

Thankfully Platt didn't make a big deal of it. Instead, he grabbed one of the top bags and, keeping it inside the Dumpster, started unwinding the plastic tie.

Julia took a bag and simply ripped open a hole. She yanked out a handful and suddenly found her gag reflex starting to betray her. She hated that she actually had to swallow back the bile. Damn, she never got nauseated. Why now? Especially when she didn't want Benjamin Platt going back and telling Maggie that her tough-as-nails friend flipped her cookies over a pile of schoolkids' leftovers.

"Do you want any of the bags the lettuce came in?" She tried to concentrate on the task at hand. The discarded lettuce bags were the only things she was holding that she could recognize. Everything else was a mish-mash of brown sludge that already smelled bad.

"Yeah, that'd be great."

Platt set aside his own garbage bag to take one of the lettuce bags.

"There are codes printed on the seam." He pulled a bag apart and showed her. "The produce companies put these codes in place after the spinach recall in 2006. Let's see if I can remember how this works. This bag's code is P227A. The first letter identifies the processing plant, the 227 is the two hundred and twenty-seventh day of the year, and the last letter usually refers to which shift bagged it. Now they keep records at the plant so we can track which supplier and hopefully even which field provided that day's lettuce."

"We've got like forty or fifty empty lettuce bags here. Do you want all of them?"

Julia swore she saw his shoulders slump at the enormity

of the project. He shoved his shirtsleeves up above his elbows not noticing that he had gotten some of the brown sludge on them. His eyes scanned the sky as if looking for answers.

Finally he shrugged and said, "We have to start somewhere."

TWENTY-EIGHT

NEBRASKA

Maggie hadn't thought about what she'd say to Johnny Bosh to convince him to leave his safe haven. She also hadn't given much thought to how she would drag his six-foot, 180-pound frame back through the tight squeeze. Now none of that mattered, at least not to the point of urgency. She'd leave it to the paramedics or rescue crew to figure out.

She sat with him for a good ten minutes, all too conscious of the fact that she was more comfortable with dead victims than with the living. She hadn't had a single answer for Dawson Hayes back at the hospital when he proclaimed that she should have left him to die with the others.

She should have predicted that after such a tragedy, the survivors would have a difficult time. If she hadn't predicted it as a profiler of human behavior, she should have known from personal experience. How many times had she survived at the hands of a killer while others had died?

It wasn't even a year ago that Kyle Cunningham had died after being exposed to the Ebola virus. Maggie had been exposed, too. Not a week went by that she didn't ask herself why she had survived and Cunningham hadn't.

The real professionals—like her best friend Gwen Patterson, who dealt with the psychological behavior of the living on a daily basis—were quick to identify it as survivor's guilt: that constant tendency to question instead of accept or simply feel grateful. Maggie could understand that, but not suicide.

"What was it that made you do this?" she asked Johnny, sitting across from him, leaning against the cold cinder-block support column and staring into his dead eyes.

Dust motes floated in the halo from her penlight. The only sound came from the earbuds of his iPod, the tiny gadget tucked into his shirt pocket. It was hip hop or rap, more words than music. That's why she had mistaken the sound for Johnny mumbling to himself.

Maybe he hadn't intended to kill himself. It was possible he just wanted to escape, forget about everything and everyone for a few hours. She didn't see any drug paraphernalia. There was nothing in the dirt surrounding him.

That's when she saw the cell phone still clamped in his hand. Had he called someone?

She easily tugged the phone away. Rigor mortis hadn't fully set in yet. With the penlight she looked for the On switch. Pressed it. Nothing. Pressed again and held it down, but the phone still didn't come on. The battery might need recharging. She slipped it deep into the front pocket of her jeans.

Maggie finally turned herself around and started to leave. It would be easier getting out than it had been coming in. Less surprises. It would be good to breathe some fresh air, to stand up straight and stretch. And yet, she hesitated. She knew she was headed for more unfamiliar ground as soon as she crawled out from under this house. And that's what made her hesitate.

She sat back on her haunches and looked at Johnny Bosh again.

"What the hell am I supposed to tell your mom?"

TWENTY-NINE

Mary Ellen Wychulis didn't have to wait this time. Irene Baldwin stood in the doorway and waved Mary Ellen into her office as she got off the elevator.

Inside, a television blared from a cabinet Mary Ellen had never seen opened. Her boss silenced the TV with a remote as she marched by and then dropped into her chair. There were no commands this time for Mary Ellen to sit but she took her usual place and stayed at the edge of her seat.

"Why am I hearing about a possible food contamination in one of our schools—one of our District schools—from CNN?"

"No one from the school notified us."

"I've made half a dozen phone calls and no one seems to know what's going on. Someone from the CDC," she said as she flipped scribbled pages of her legal pad, "a Roger Bix, told me that he put in a request with us two days ago about

155

another contamination in a Norfolk, Virginia, high school. He was told that we would have to assess the situation and get back to him. I don't remember getting this request and I know I didn't talk to this man. I would certainly remember such a condescending voice."

Mary Ellen kept her hands still when her first impulse was to wring them in her lap.

"Did you talk to Roger Bix?" her boss asked.

Mary Ellen fielded dozens of calls and even more emails every day: requests, applications, complaints. Many of them were taken by her secretary. How could she be expected to remember every single one without first checking? But she remembered Bix.

"Yes, and I highly recommended that he speak to Undersecretary Eisler. His department oversees the NSLP." She stopped, but then, because she knew Baldwin hated acronyms, quickly added, "The National School Lunch Program. I also forwarded him the paperwork necessary to determine whether or not this particular situation warranted an assessment by the Strategic Partnership Program Agroterrorism."

"Agroterrorism? He called it an act of terrorism?"

"He insinuated that the contamination might be intentional."

"So he called requesting our assistance for what he believed to be an intentional contamination in a public high school and you sent him forms to fill out?"

"It's standard procedure for an assessment to be made. I also referred him to Undersecretary Eisler."

Baldwin shook her head and Mary Ellen steeled herself for a lecture. Instead her boss said, "Can we simply pull the inspection records for these two schools? See if any of them have been cited or warned? Cross-check to see if they've used the same supplier?"

"We'd need to request the inspection records from the state of Virginia and the District of Columbia."

"Isn't the USDA responsible for inspecting school cafeterias and kitchens?"

"We oversee the NSLP, but we don't actually have those records."

"Okay, what do we *actually* have then?"

It was late. Mary Ellen didn't have the patience for another round of her boss's sarcastic remarks. She just wanted to go home to her beautiful baby and doting husband. That schoolkids had gotten sick was unfortunate but it happened. Kids were notorious virus magnets. Roger Bix sounded like a condescending prick. Even Baldwin thought so. Mary Ellen got tired of the CDC pushing their weight around, thinking they were superior to any other government agency.

"Wychulis?"

Mary Ellen realized she had waited too long to explain. It was a complex procedure, one she already knew her boss would not appreciate.

"The state keeps track of every district," Mary Ellen began. "We require each school, in order to comply with the NSLP and be a part of the program, to have their facilities inspected twice a year. The states report the number of schools inspected but they don't report the school names."

Baldwin stared at her, for once speechless.

"I believe the undersecretary for food and nutrition is directly responsible for the NSLP," Mary Ellen repeated, losing count of how many times she had already said this. "I'm sure Mr. Eisler would be able to explain the process much more accurately."

Then she pursed her lips, trying to confine her irritation. She folded her hands in her lap and stopped herself from adding that this should be Eisler's mess.

"I've offered our conference room," Baldwin said, "for a task force strategy and information center. I'm hoping Mr. Bix will agree to use it, so we can maintain some control. He already has personnel from the FBI, DHS, the District police department, and USAMRIID on the case."

"USAMRIID? That seems a bit reactionary, doesn't it?"

"Considering he believes it might be intentional, I'd say it's rather smart. I get the impression Mr. Bix is good at dotting his i's and crossing his t's. Speaking of which, we'll need to have a meeting first thing in the morning with our people. Please contact the necessary members. I would prefer we keep this confined to essential personnel only."

"Yes, of course. What about the media?" Mary Ellen asked.

"Mr. Bix has agreed that no one talks to anyone until we know what's going on." She flipped the pages of her legal pad, again, until she found what she wanted. Then she ripped out two pages. "Here's a list of what we'll need set up in the conference room for our meeting with Mr. Bix."

Mary Ellen took the pages noticing the list was single-spaced, double columns. "I'll see to it that everything is there first thing in the morning."

"See to it that everything is set up immediately."

"Immediately?"

"Bix and his team will be arriving in about two hours."

THIRTY

—

NEBRASKA

Maggie couldn't remember the last time she was more relieved to see anyone. Donny stood on the sidewalk out of the way of the rescue crew and the bystanders. Still hearing Mrs. Bosh's sobs, Maggie retreated to stand alongside him.

"I brought your car," he said, keeping his eyes on the people trampling the Boshes' carefully manicured lawn.

She glanced down the street and recognized her rented Toyota in the line of vehicles.

"How did you know I was here?"

"The whole county knows you're here."

She wasn't quite sure why, but that simple statement of fact felt like a punch to her gut.

"I should have known something like this would happen," she said under her breath, by no means a confession but rather an admonishment to herself.

"We all should have known."

They stood silent and still while the world seemed to spin around them.

Maggie was struck by how different the crowd was from what she was used to. There were a few gawkers but mostly it looked like friends and neighbors huddled together, comforting the Boshes. Neighbors raced off to bring back ropes or twine, garden clippers and other tools from their sheds or garages, anything that might help the rescue crew which worked with an urgent steadiness despite making a recovery instead of a rescue.

Maggie understood now why they had all come last night. It wasn't to exert their authority and see firsthand what was happening. Mostly it had been to help. That's what they were used to doing, chipping in and helping each other.

"Thanks for bringing the car," she told Donny.

"Not a problem. We explained to the rental branch in Scottsbluff, and they gave us an extra key." He dug in his pocket and handed her the set. "The manager also adjusted your rate in the computer. Said they'll only charge you for the weekend but you wouldn't need to return it until late next week if need be."

"Good deal. The State Patrol discount?"

"We do what we can." He tipped his hat and finally allowed a smile. "One catch, I do need a ride back to North Platte. Figured you'd want to be there for the autopsies. That is unless you're headed back to Denver."

She hadn't heard from Kunze, but then she hadn't exactly been checking for messages. It'd be easier to simply hand this investigation over and leave. Donny and the State Patrol were more than capable. She could be in Denver before nightfall, check into the hotel, take a hot shower, order room service, and be rested and ready to teach her sessions tomorrow and Sunday. No one would question her decision. Skylar would probably welcome her absence.

She saw him glance in her direction. Earlier he'd helped her out from under the porch, but when she delivered the news, he'd stepped away, shaking his head as if it were somehow her fault.

She watched the Boshes, holding each other up, waiting while the rescue crew organized their efforts. Maggie was almost certain toxicology would show an overdose of some form of drug. There'd be no need to spend the county's budget on another autopsy. Yes, Denver was starting to sound like a good idea. After the autopsies of the other two boys.

She asked Donny to drive her to North Platte.

"Maybe we can stop at the convenience store before we head out," he said as they climbed into the Toyota.

"Yes, I could use a Diet Pepsi."

"Your suitcase is in the trunk."

"Thanks."

"The store out by the highway has a nice, roomy bathroom."

This time she turned and stared at him.

"Investigator Fergussen, are you saying I stink?"

She noticed the back of his neck flush.

"Just offering a suggestion."

Of course it was in the convenience store's "nice, roomy," single-room bathroom shortly after Maggie had removed her dirty clothes—all of her clothes—that the call came in from Assistant Director Kunze. She thought about pressing Ignore and making him leave a voice message. She already knew what he would say. But instead, she checked the door's lock and grabbed the cell phone.

"This is Maggie O'Dell."

"Please tell me, Agent O'Dell, that you are either in Denver or on your way there."

"I've had a bit of a delay." She had given him the basics in her voice message.

"I'm sure the local authorities appreciate your efforts and are more than capable of taking over."

"One of the surviving teenagers just committed suicide."

She wasn't sure why she blurted it out. Old habits were hard to break. It was something she would have done naturally with Cunningham. He would have responded with something brisk but profound. A reassurance that they were the good guys and that he knew she had done everything possible. He had been their boss, their leader, and he gave his agents hell when they deserved it but he also took care of them. She hadn't realized how much she counted on him until he was gone.

She was thinking about this while waiting for Kunze to

criticize, to lecture, to humiliate her. But he said something totally unexpected.

"How can I protect you if you constantly keep getting yourself into these messes?"

"Excuse me? What exactly do you think you're protecting me from?"

Even as she said it, she examined herself in the bathroom mirror. Under the stark fluorescent lights the scar on her abdomen and the one on her side seemed to pucker up, betraying her. Dirt from underneath the Boshes' house smudged her face. Remnants of cobwebs still tangled her hair. She had rubbed holes in her shirtsleeves and her elbows were caked with blood and dirt from crawling. Okay, perhaps at this moment she did look a bit frazzled, but she was not someone who needed protecting.

She realized Kunze was silent and wondered if she had lost the connection just as she heard him sigh.

"You have three sessions at the Denver law enforcement conference starting tomorrow."

"Any seasoned police detective who's gone through Quantico's training could substitute for me."

"But I didn't send any police detective. I sent you. Please make sure those attendees are not sitting there without an instructor. I'll see you on Monday, Agent O'Dell."

"Actually I fly back on Monday."

"I'll see you on Tuesday morning, Agent O'Dell."

She heard the click, and then silence. Typical Kunze, he ended his calls as abruptly as he began them.

Minutes ago she had made the same decision as her boss had. Why did she argue? Was it his statement about protecting her? What the hell did he mean by that?

Ever since Kunze replaced Cunningham he had been riding her, questioning her, sending her into killers' warehouses and into the path of a hurricane. He had bluntly told her that he thought her negligence had contributed to Cunningham's death and that she would need to prove herself to him. But how many times did she have to do it?

In just the last year, she had solved a major piece of the puzzle to a bombing at Mall of America. But it had placed her and Kunze on opposite sides of a political fallout. Then last month she had survived a category-5 hurricane only to uncover a ploy that made the U.S. Navy look bad. Again, tripping up her politically correct and politically connected new boss. Whatever happened to doing the right thing, no matter what the consequences were? Cunningham always understood. Okay, yes, sometimes he'd be mad as hell at her, but he'd understand. He might question her means but never had he questioned her intent.

She cleaned up in the small sink, doing as good a job as possible with stiff, brown paper towels that scraped the dirt off rather than wiped. Then she pulled on fresh clothes. Brushed her hair. Already she felt better.

She rolled up her dirty clothes and started shoving them into a side pocket of her suitcase when something tumbled to the floor.

Johnny's cell phone.

She had forgotten all about it. She shut the toilet lid and sat down. She remembered Dawson's eyes last night. Johnny's eyes just moments ago.

That's when she decided.

Kunze said he didn't want the conference attendees sitting there without an instructor. She would make sure they had someone.

She grabbed her cell phone and punched through her Contact menu. While in Florida last month she had met a detective from the Denver Police Department. Glen Karst was a seasoned homicide detective who had been through the criminal behavior training course at Quantico. She found his phone number and hoped he wasn't busy this weekend. She'd owe him a steak dinner, some cheesecake, and a bottle of Buffalo Trace. It seemed like a bargain.

THIRTY-ONE

―――――

"Did your techs find anything more in the forest?" Maggie asked Donny as soon as they were back on the road.

"We did find the live wire Dawson Hayes ran into. Someone must have cut it, rigged it from the fence post, and strung it between two trees."

"Like a trap."

"The fence line they took the electric wire from actually cordons off pasture land from the forest. The kid must have run into the trap wire and the shock was enough to throw him into the barbed wire. We could see where it snapped from the posts."

"And the momentum kept him rolling, taking the barbed wire and wrapping it around him."

"Yup. That's what we're thinking. We left the hotwire coiled and out of reach. I'll need to find and talk to the rancher who leases that pasture. Have him shut off the current."

"How did you touch it without getting a shock?"

"Whoever rigged it left pieces of plastic—they're sort of safety guards so you can handle it hot without getting shocked. That's why we know it was rigged on purpose. Ranchers don't use anything like that."

"Is it possible the other two boys ran into the wire, too?"

"We'll have to wait and see what Lucy says, but I'm guessing no. Not enough juice to electrocute. Just enough to knock you on your ass. Remember, ranchers just want to discourage cattle, not fry them. Sorry," he said, his ears turning red. "Didn't mean to be crude."

"I guess that's why Dawson's alive."

"The crime team also cast some of the footprints."

"So the tarps held?"

"Yeah, the tarps preserved them from the rain but I'm not sure it'll matter unless we confiscate all seven kids' shoes."

When she didn't respond he glanced at her and winced. "You want me to confiscate all seven kids' shoes?"

"We already have three pairs."

"There's one set of prints that looks like a size thirteen work boot. I don't remember any of the boys wearing anything close to a work boot."

"So it may come in handy collecting the shoes, after all."

He didn't argue.

"We did find some animal tracks up on the ridge. Rain made a mess of them. Could be a cougar. Maybe a coyote or large dog. Hard to tell."

"You're kidding?"

"Hank said there were a few sightings of a cougar reported in the last several weeks. Nothing confirmed. Still, doesn't add much to the story. None of these kids had injuries that come close to a cat attack."

"What about Amanda Vicks's arm?"

"That didn't look like an animal bite to me. I think we got a photo of it if you wanna take a look." He glanced over at her. "What's this all about?"

"Dawson Hayes said this morning that a wolflike animal came at him."

"Really?"

"Did you find any tracks down in the campsite area?"

"Not a one."

"Anything that could have produced a light show?"

He shook his head. Glanced at her again but this time it looked as if he was trying to decide how to say what he wanted to say.

"I have to tell you, I think some of those kids were stoned last night. We didn't find any bottles or cans. A few cigarette butts. No joints. But I know from their stories and that spaced-out look, it wasn't just shock and awe."

Maggie hadn't told Sheriff Skylar about the salvia because of his holding back evidence of drugs in a previous case. Allegedly he'd rather have the girl's parents believe she accidentally fell from the bridge instead of knowing she had tripped out on salvia and jumped. But she couldn't hold out on Donny.

"Lucy did find a baggie. She thinks it may be *Salvia divinorum.*"

She left it at that, letting him believe Lucy could have found it today while she prepped the two boys for autopsies.

"I thought so," Donny said, tapping the steering wheel in triumph of being correct. He didn't even question the how or when of the discovery.

"Do you know much about salvia?"

"It's a hallucinogen. I've heard it compared to LSD. Supposed to be nonaddictive with no long-term side effects. The big trend right now is with kids filming their trips, posting them on YouTube."

"You think that's what was happening last night?"

"It would certainly explain their stories, the fireworks and laser light show. I had one kid telling me how loud the purple was."

"We didn't find a camera, though," Maggie said.

"Nope. No camera."

"And isn't it a little strange that they would all see fireworks and a light show?"

"Kids are easily influenced. The drug might make them more impressionable. If one kid claimed he saw fireworks, maybe they all thought they did."

Maggie noticed they had driven for miles on the rolling ribbon of two-lane asphalt and yet they hadn't crossed a single intersection. The only breaks were a few long driveways to ranches or farms or cutouts to pastures. She couldn't help thinking that even in the middle of nowhere these kids knew about salvia and were able to purchase it illegally. Donny was right. Teenagers were easily influenced and not much different no matter where they lived.

"If we're right," Maggie said, "chances are this wasn't their first trip, so to speak, in the forest. Can we get ahold of Trevor's and Kyle's text messages and their computers?"

"I can probably do that."

"When we were looking at the cattle mutilation ... " Maggie started but paused. Was it only yesterday? "Nolan Comstock mentioned lights in the night sky. Said people were used to seeing them."

She watched as Donny's jaw twitched.

"He didn't seem to be a crazy, old rancher," she said, choosing the two adjectives that Skylar had used to describe Lucy. "Do people see lights in the night sky? And if so, what are they?"

He was quiet for a while then said, "We really are smack-dab between two major air force installations. It's no secret they fly maneuvers over this part of the country. They probably test drive all kinds of strange new technology. And of course, they're not going to be announcing it or admitting it."

"Any chance that's what these kids saw? Some sort of clandestine war game."

"No. The government wouldn't purposely hurt kids." He looked offended by the idea.

She didn't push it. She wasn't sure she believed it, but she needed Donny Fergussen on her side. She remembered the look Sheriff Skylar had given her when she told them Johnny Bosh was dead. There was something about it that made Maggie realize a lot of people would be taking sides before all this was over.

THIRTY-TWO

WASHINGTON, D.C.

Benjamin Platt carried a hard-shell case filled with an assortment of samples. He was anxious to get back to a lab at USAMRIID. Bix had overnighted a set to his CDC scientists in Atlanta as well. Platt would, no doubt, be cross-checking what Bix's experts had looked for at the Norfolk high school, including a variety of strains of E. coli and salmonella along with norovirus and a few other sneaky bacteria. He also had more than a dozen baggies filled with leftovers and garbage that he and Julia Racine had carefully scavenged.

He was still smiling at Julia's last remark: "I've never seen a guy get so excited about vomit. Your mother must be very proud."

She stood beside him now, shoulder holster in full view as if providing backup while he loaded the samples into his Land Rover. They ignored the media that had followed, tossing questions and sticking microphones in their faces. That's when Racine pushed back her jacket to show her badge as well as her firearm. She shoved one reporter off the curb then held out her hand like a running back, strong-arming anyone else who dared get in their way.

Finally inside the vehicle, Platt was ready to make a get-away. He revved the engine to warn the Channel 5 news crew at his hood that he wouldn't hesitate to roll over them. He accelerated forward, braked hard. Watched the big guy with a camera jump-step out of his way. Suddenly the back door to the Land Rover opened. Racine turned ready to pounce over the seat. Roger Bix slid inside.

"Go," Bix said. "Run these assholes over if you have to."

Halfway down the street Platt said, "I'm taking Detective Racine to her car. You want me to take you to yours?"

"USDA just invited us over to their house to play a game of information swap."

"Really? I thought they had to assess your request."

"Evidently they've assessed it. My guess, our new Miss Undersecretary watched a little television this afternoon and is now as nervous as a long-tail cat in a room full of rocking chairs."

Platt glanced at Racine then at Bix in the rearview mirror. Bix was finally slipping back to his old self, using metaphors that would still sound ridiculous even without the Southern drawl.

"So you want me to drop you off at the Department of Agriculture?"

"Drop me off? I thought we were in this together. Like Batman and Robin or the Lone Ranger and Tonto."

Platt bit back: "More like Archie and Jughead," and added, "Believe me, Roger, I'm more useful to you in a research lab, hunting for what made these kids sick. Not in some office, sipping tea, eating finger food, and batting around political mumbo-jumbo."

"Actually you're both coming with me. I need a show of force."

"What happened to Agent Tully?"

"His boss said there wasn't enough information yet to make this an FBI matter." Bix pursed his lips and muttered, "Bastard."

"Officially, I'm not assigned to this case either," Racine told him.

Bix held up his cell phone. "Who do I need to call to get you officially assigned?"

"Roger, this is her day off. What the hell's going on with you?"

"Only twenty minutes," Bix promised.

"Sure, why not. I'm hungry."

Before Platt could argue, Bix's cell phone started playing something that sounded more like salsa when Platt would have expected country western. The guy was full of surprises.

Bix glanced at the caller ID, frowned, then shook his head as he answered, "This is Bix." He listened for several seconds and finally said, "Yes, of course, I believe you. I never said I didn't believe you."

Platt exchanged looks with Julia but stayed quiet. He continued to shoot glances at the rearview mirror, watching Bix. The man appeared visibly shaken, eyes darting outside the vehicle windows as if trying to locate his caller someplace on the sidewalks of the District. Was that sweat on his upper lip?

"Christ almighty, you cannot be serious." It came out as a hiss of disbelief rather than anger. "You've got to give me more than that to go on. Hold on. Wait a minute." He brought the phone down and stared at it before he slapped it shut. The person had hung up before Bix was finished.

He wiped a sleeve across his sweaty face and then said, "There's going to be more schools."

He said it so quietly Platt wasn't sure he heard him correctly.

"What do you mean, going to be?" Julia asked.

"If we don't figure this out by Monday morning then Monday afternoon there'll be more sick kids."

"Who did you just talk to, Roger?"

"I don't know."

"Is this some food terrorist plot?" Julia asked.

"Almost as bad," Bix said. "But not a terrorist. A whistle-blower."

THIRTY-THREE

NEBRASKA

Since North Platte was an hour and a half away, Maggie called and told Lucy not to wait. She had finished the autopsy on one boy and was doing an external examination of the second when Donny and Maggie walked in.

Maggie had to admit, she was impressed with the autopsy suite, a bright, gleaming pathology lab in the basement of the community hospital. After discovering the archaism of Nebraska's coroner system, she wasn't sure what to expect.

Last night Lucy had tried to explain how Nebraska law required the county attorney to also be the coroner, which put prosecutors across the state in charge of each county's death investigations. It was a ninety-year-old law that set few standards, leaving it up to individual county attorneys to determine if and when an investigation even took place. No medical training was necessary. Death investigation training, which amounted to a day down in Lincoln, was optional. At one time Lucy Coy was the only professionally trained medical examiner in a five-county area.

"You have to understand," Lucy had said last night, "Nebraska has about 1.6 million people in the entire state and a million of them live within a fifty-mile radius of Omaha and Lincoln. Both cities, of course, have their own medical examiners and homicide departments. Lincoln has the State Patrol Crime Lab. Omaha has the Douglas County Regional Crime Lab. They have all the high-tech luxuries, you might say, of a metropolitan city, but that's also where most of the crimes happen. In this part of the state it isn't like people are stabbed or shot to death every week. It just isn't necessary to have all the technology and specialties."

"Unless it's your family or friend who winds up dead out here in the middle of the Sandhills," Maggie had countered.

"It's been said before"—Lucy had shrugged—"that if you want to get away with murder, western Nebraska would be a good place to try it."

When Donny had given Maggie his geography lesson yesterday, she hadn't quite translated what that sort of isolation could mean. Today she was beginning to understand firsthand.

She was, however, relieved to finally have some familiar surroundings. Even the scrub gowns were the same—two sizes too large, which Maggie always believed was on purpose to reduce guests to a more vulnerable state. Sometimes law enforcement officers required a bit of humility to relate to the victim. But Donny's gown stretched tight across his barrel chest. The shoe covers didn't quite make it all the way up his heels.

Lucy had her hands on Kyle Bandor's ankle, her long fingers in purple latex. She looked up at Maggie.

"I heard what happened," she said. "Are you all right?"

"You already heard about Johnny Bosh?"

"Unfortunately bad news travels fast. Oliver Cushman will be doing the death investigation."

"County Attorney Cushman? The man I sent away last night."

"Yes."

"Wonderful. Will he even order an autopsy?"

"For a suicide?" Lucy looked to Donny for the answer but he shrugged. "Probably not," she said. "He'll probably order a toxicology report." She glanced back at Maggie. "How did he look?"

"Dead," Maggie said bluntly, avoiding Lucy's eyes, suddenly aware of them studying her with genuine concern. She didn't like the fact that if she closed her eyes right now she would still see Johnny Bosh staring at her.

"I didn't see any drug paraphernalia," Maggie explained. "His skin wasn't red like it can be from certain poisons. His eyes were bloodshot but it didn't look like petechial hemorrhage, so whatever he took didn't strangle or asphyxiate him. I didn't smell or see any vomit. His mother told us she noticed some OxyContin missing from her medicine cabinet."

"Depending on how many he ingested and if he crushed

them ... most likely he suffered a cardiac arrest. Was there a note?" Lucy asked.

"If there was, no one's found it yet." Maggie remembered the boy's cell phone in the side pocket of her suitcase. She was hoping it might offer some clues. Later she'd figure out if she could recharge it and take a look before handing it back to the family or—cringe—to County Attorney Cushman.

"Well, let me share what I've found so far."

Lucy left Kyle with a soft double tap to his chest as though telling the boy she would be right back. Maggie was struck by the intimacy of the gesture. She'd watched dozens of medical examiners, coroners, and pathologists in her ten years as a federal agent and during her forensic fellowship. She believed it took a special personality to work with the dead, to slice tissue, pluck off maggots, suck out brains, and section apart organs, reducing the human body to bits and pieces all in an effort to solve a mystery, tell a story, and hopefully reveal secrets that even the killer couldn't hide.

In Maggie's experience the MEs and their counterparts were detail-oriented, efficient problem solvers, thinkers not feelers. They didn't personalize their surgical procedures even while showing and demanding respect for the victim. She couldn't count the number of times she'd watched a medical examiner stare down a visiting law enforcement officer who, in his own discomfort with the procedure, had made an off-color remark.

But there was something different in the way Lucy

conducted business in an autopsy suite. Maggie watched as Lucy pulled a sheet off the first boy—the sheet, in and of itself, was a courtesy rarely used at this stage.

"Trevor displayed external signs of electrocution. He's the one we examined in the forest." She gently took his right foot in her hands, turning it slowly as if not to disturb the boy and showing the extent of the damage.

In the forest, Maggie had noticed that Trevor's high-top sneaker had been blown off his right foot, leaving a smudge of black on his sock. Now with no shoe or sock she could see the broken blood vessels at the top of his foot and the charred leathery burn at the bottom.

"In cases of electrocution," Lucy said, placing his foot down and going to the other end of the stainless-steel table, "the electrical current has a source point. Often the head or hands. In Trevor's case it was up at his left shoulder." She pointed at the obvious wound where the skin puckered red, swollen, and blistered. "The current passes through the body, usually taking the path of least resistance, choosing nerves and tissue rather than skin. The ground point is often the feet."

She waved them closer to take a look inside his chest cavity. Maggie noticed Lucy hadn't removed any of Trevor's organs yet.

"Muscles contract," she continued. "The nervous system goes haywire. Temporary paralysis results. And depending how high the voltage, organs, including the brain, can hemorrhage. As you can see."

Donny had slid his hands into his trouser pockets. Without his Stetson Maggie thought he looked disarmed. But he didn't seem fazed by any of this.

"This definitely wasn't a Taser," he said.

"No. Definitely not a Taser."

"Any idea where the electrical current came from?" he asked.

"Take a closer look at the source point."

Lucy's purple-gloved finger traced over the shoulder wound. "Are either of you familiar with how lasers cut?"

She paused as Donny and Maggie exchanged a glance. The question seemed to come out of left field. Lucy didn't wait for an answer.

"Lasers actually cut by burning or breaking apart molecules that bond tissue together. It looks like Trevor was initially cut when the electrical current hit his shoulder. Take a look." She stood back. "It cauterizes the cuts automatically so there's no blood."

"You're suggesting these two boys were hit and electrocuted by a laser beam?" Maggie asked. She didn't bother to hide her skepticism.

"It would need to be a very intense laser pulse. But yes, that's what I believe hit them."

"And it just came out of the sky?"

"Or maybe a laser stun gun," Donny said.

"Is there such a thing?"

"It uses a laser beam to ionize, if that's the correct term." Lucy nodded and he continued. "The ionized air produces sort of threadlike filaments of glowing plasma from the gun to the target. Supposedly you can sweep a lightning-like beam of electricity across a wide area. I can't remember how many feet away. They call it a shock rifle. It can interrupt a vehicle's electronic ignition system and stop it cold."

"That would certainly explain the light show the kids talked about," Maggie said. "But I don't know of any available weapon like that. Are you sure you're not just reading too many science digests, Investigator Fergussen?"

"Oh there're available but there's only one place I know of that would have them."

"And where might that be?"

"The United States Department of Defense."

THIRTY-FOUR

Platt and Bix trailed behind Julia and their security escort to the third-floor conference room. Julia was still complaining about having to leave her weapon. Platt took the opportunity to whisper to Bix, "What's the game plan, Roger?"

"Just follow my lead. This is solely to gather information."

"No task force?"

"Like I'm gonna trust them."

"Do you have a choice?"

"Watch me." Then he let his guard down and confessed, "I really need you to back me up."

Earlier, on the drive over to Fourteenth Street and Independence Avenue, Platt had made Bix talk, threatening he'd drop him in the middle of a District intersection to walk if he continued to withhold information.

Truth was, Bix knew very little. Earlier that morning,

someone who claimed to have insider knowledge told him there would be more schools. It would be the exact scenario as the Norfolk, Virginia, contamination. They'd find the same bacteria. Kids would get very sick. Some would be hospitalized. There might even be fatalities. When Bix demanded to know who the person was, he hung up.

At first Platt wondered if it might be a reporter. Someone guessing, hedging his bets, creating a bigger story by being a part of the story. Maybe the man had simply made a lucky guess. But why call again and risk being wrong? Bix insisted the person told him specific details that only an insider would know. Platt, however, wasn't convinced.

The conference room looked suspiciously big for gathering information. Platt had been in other situations like this—or at least, what he imagined this to be—with government officials acting more like politicians than public servants, working their asses off to save their asses. If past experience was any indication, the plush conference room, reserved for catered meetings that required leather high-back chairs and big-screen presentations, was more for intimidation.

As soon as their security escort left, Julia immediately headed for the refreshment table. Bix grabbed a can of Pepsi and popped it open. Gulped almost half the can. Platt didn't think Bix would be able to pull this off as long as his upper lip remained sweaty.

"What do you know about this person you're calling a whistle-blower? If what he's saying is true, we have just over forty-eight hours to figure out what's going on. Do you even know he's for real?"

"I know enough to realize if there's another attack the USDA is not going to come out smelling like a bouquet."

"Rose."

"Excuse me?"

"Never mind," Platt said. The man's awkward metaphors shouldn't make a difference right now, even if they got on Platt's nerves. "You think the USDA is somehow responsible?"

"This is what I know: Yesterday when I asked for their help they had no interest in doing anything more than sending me from one department to another. Today they invite me here for a strategy session."

"Is that what they called it? A strategy session?"

"I don't give a damn what they called it. You're missing the point, Platt. Today every media outlet was on the scene and oh, by the way, now suddenly the USDA wants to help."

Platt couldn't argue. Government agencies had a tendency to be reactive instead of proactive. But their timing didn't necessarily mean they had something to hide. At the same time, he couldn't shake the fact that someone had followed him from his meeting at the diner with Bix all the way to his parents' home.

"Would you recognize this so-called whistle-blower's voice if you met him?"

Bix shook his head. "He uses a computer voice."

"What do you mean?"

"You know, where you key in your words on a computer and the program reads it out loud. Sort of like the mechanical voice that says, 'You've got mail.'"

"So maybe he *is* concerned you'd recognize his real voice."

"Too many veggies." Julia returned with a plate full. "I'm so sick of people telling me what's good for me," she said as she crunched a celery stick. "Department of Agriculture, hmpf. You'd think they'd provide a few chunks of meat. Have you ordered a trace on the cell-phone call?"

"I tried this morning. It's a secure number."

"There're usually ways to get around that."

Both men stared at her, waiting to hear what she meant when a woman came into the conference room. She wore a flowered silk blouse under a fitted blazer with a skirt that accentuated her willowy figure making her appear softer and betraying her stickler personality. She was attractive with wavy brown hair that fell past her shoulders and green eyes that sparked slightly with irritation as soon as she saw Platt. She was tall, almost as tall as him but mostly because she insisted on wearing three-inch spiked heels, which he knew she hated and was reminded how much when she walked across the long conference room.

She offered her hand to Bix first.

"You must be Roger Bix. I'm Mary Ellen Wychulis."

"This is Julia Racine and—"

"And Colonel Benjamin Platt," she interrupted Bix and didn't even bother to glance at Julia.

"You know each other." Bix sounded almost as surprised as Platt was. He didn't think he knew anyone at the USDA.

"Yes," Mary Ellen said. "Ben and I know each other."

"I didn't know you worked here," Platt said.

Bix looked at him as if seeing a traitor. He was waiting for an explanation. Even Julia had bristled, her eyes darting between the two of them.

"Mary Ellen and I used to be married."

THIRTY-FIVE

NEBRASKA

"There was blood," Lucy explained as she pointed to a black T-shirt on a stainless-steel tray. "Kyle's shirt but it's not his blood."

"One of the other kid's?" Maggie asked thinking about Dawson and the bloody mess he had been when she stumbled over him.

Lucy had started Kyle's autopsy and was focused on cutting through his ribs.

"Black dye plays havoc with DNA," Lucy said without stopping work. "No one's really sure why. But this time it won't matter. It's not any of the other teenagers' blood."

"How can you be so certain?"

"Because it's not human."

"What the hell?" Donny went to look at the shirt.

"It's pig's blood."

"You think it came with the kids or with whoever shot at them?"

"Those are the details I leave up to you investigators."

"If these kids were experimenting with salvia they might have been doing some other weird crap," Donny said.

"Like mutilating cattle?" Maggie asked.

"I said pig's blood, not cow's. We used pig's blood to re-create crime scenes in forensic training. It's close enough to human blood and easier to obtain." Lucy smiled but still didn't look up. "Donny mentioned that's what he dragged you out here for. The cattle mutilations."

"Is it possible these kids had something to do with them? Some freaky ritualistic stuff?" Maggie asked. If a county sheriff could keep it secret that area teenagers were experimenting with new and different drugs, could he keep under wraps their other illegal activities as well?

"The mutilations are too advanced and deliberate," Donny said. "Especially for a bunch of teenagers tripping on drugs. How would they figure out how to drain the blood? And erase footprints? I'd sooner believe UFO guys like Stotter than think a bunch of kids were able to pull that off."

"I have to agree," Lucy said. "About a year ago I was asked to do a necropsy on a mutilated steer. The incisions were precise as were the organs they chose to extract."

Suddenly her hands were still. She stood up straight and looked from Maggie to Donny and back. "Actually I remember thinking at the time that the incisions looked as though they had been cauterized. It would certainly explain why there's no blood. Now that I think back, it reminded me of laser surgery."

The three of them stared at one another.

"I think I need to go upstairs and talk to Dawson Hayes again," Maggie said. "There're too many strange questions left unanswered."

Donny walked her back to the rental car. He needed to retrieve his jacket and she wanted to grab hers before going back up to see Dawson, having learned that the cold invaded as soon as the sun went down. They were discussing what trace evidence Donny would send with the State Patrol technicians headed back to Lincoln. Neither of them noticed the cracked windshield until they opened the Toyota's doors.

"What the hell?" Donny was the first to see the fist-size rock on the hood.

Maggie couldn't believe it. Instinctively her head swiveled and her eyes darted around the parking lot as if she would still be able to locate the culprit.

"I thought the heartland was supposed to be a friendly place."

"People are edgy about this case."

"So why take it out on me? I'm trying to solve the crime."

"Maybe somebody doesn't want it solved."

"Then why aren't they threatening you?"

"It's against the law to threaten a State Patrol officer."

"It's against the law to threaten a federal agent." Maggie heard the frustration spilling out in her voice.

"It's easier to blame an outsider. They know I'm not going anywhere. They probably think they can convince you to pack up and go home. Don't take it personally."

"Are you serious?" She grabbed the rock and held it up. "You don't want me to take *this* personally?"

"You get used to it after a while," a man said from behind them.

Maggie spun around again. She hadn't noticed the stranger who must have come out of one of the buildings. He stood beside a Buick station wagon parked behind the Toyota. Maybe he had been waiting inside his vehicle for them.

"Name's Wesley Stotter." He put out his hand to Maggie.

"Stotter," Donny said. "The UFO guy?"

The man shrugged. "I guess some people call me that. I prefer the term 'paranormal investigator.'"

Immediately Donny winced. Maggie looked from one man to the other for an explanation.

"You're the one getting the ranchers all riled up about alien spaceships mutilating their cattle."

Stotter was about Maggie's height, thick-chested, bald-headed with violet-colored eyes and a well-manicured silver beard that made him look more like a history professor than a UFO nut.

"I saw something in the forest last night that I think you two might be interested in hearing about."

"You were there last night?" Maggie was interested now.

"I tried to come up through the back entrance. A bright beam of light stopped me about halfway up."

"You mean you stopped to watch the lights?" Donny didn't sound convinced.

"No, I said it stopped me. Literally. Shut down my car's entire electrical system."

THIRTY-SIX

Wesley Stotter knew they would be skeptical. Most law enforcement officials dismissed whatever he had to say, but what if something he saw could help their investigation? So he stuck to the facts as he told State Patrolman Fergussen and Agent O'Dell about his drive up into the forest last night.

"What are you doing out here in the Sandhills?" Fergussen wanted to know. "I thought your radio show was based in Denver."

Stotter couldn't help but be impressed that the man actually knew a little something about him.

"Chasing lights in the sky."

He watched the two investigators exchange a glance.

"I've been examining cattle mutilations for years now," he explained. "You've had a string of them recently. Seven, to be exact, within twenty-three days."

Fergussen crossed his arms and shook his head, but now Agent O'Dell seemed interested.

"You think the lights have something to do with it?" she asked.

"When you've looked at dozens of cattle mutilations you can't deny the similarities. Seeing lights in the night sky before or after is common."

"And that leads you to believe alien spacecrafts are involved?"

He studied her for a moment, not sure if she was playing with him or genuinely interested. Up until this point Fergussen had asked all the questions while O'Dell busied herself with a salad she had piled high from the hospital's cafeteria.

They had found a table in the corner where no one could hear them. Fergussen had picked up a sandwich. Stotter grabbed a doughnut and coffee. O'Dell was the only one devouring her food. Stotter was a bit surprised at her appetite. He knew they had just come from viewing the autopsies of the dead boys.

"Not necessarily alien," he finally admitted.

"That's right," Fergussen said. "You've got the ranchers all up in arms believing some conspiracy with black ops helicopters is responsible for killing their cattle."

"The government's been secretly testing bovine parts for years, although I doubt they'd ever admit it. Back in the '80s they snatched up thyroid glands, paying meat-processing plants and butchers top dollar. Nobody knew what the hell they were doing with them nor did anyone care.

"Then all of a sudden Uncle Sam was done and the

processing plants were flooded with bovine thyroid glands. So what did they do with them? They ground them up with hamburger until tens of thousands got sick with something called thyrotoxicosis."

O'Dell stopped with her fork in midair and asked Fergussen, "Is that true?"

Fergussen stared at him without answering.

Stotter realized he needed to be careful. He couldn't go off on tangents like he did on his radio show. Most people didn't want to hear this stuff. It was one of the reasons the government got away with what it did.

"Consider the parts that are consistently taken in almost every single cattle mutilation," Stotter tried again. "Jaws are stripped to the bone. Reproductive organs, tongues, digestive tracks, all removed. The blood completely drained. Think about it. The jaw has saliva glands. The digestive track absorbs and collects traces of chemicals or toxins. Even the ears act as a filter. If you were doing tests on animals and didn't want anyone to know, you'd remove all the bodily fluids and all the pieces that might hold clues that could give you away."

"So they use a helicopter to snatch a cow up out of a herd," Fergussen said, arms still crossed and Stotter could see he didn't believe him. "Where exactly do they perform all these tests? In the air?"

"Have you ever heard of a mobile slaughter unit?" He could see Fergussen had. O'Dell shook her head. "The USDA provides these state-of-the-art butcher shops on

wheels. They're part of a farm initiative, an outreach program for rural areas."

"Yeah, what about it?"

"I've seen the mobile slaughter units in the same areas
that have had cattle mutilations."

"Coincidence," Fergussen said, only now he grew impa-
tient, sitting up, ready to cut this short. "So which is it,
Stotter? Government conspiracy or alien spaceship?"

"What makes you think it has to be one or the other?"

"I've had enough," Fergussen said but looked over at
O'Dell.

"What does any of this have to do with two dead
teenagers?" she asked.

"Maybe they saw something they weren't supposed to
see."

THIRTY-SEVEN

————

WASHINGTON, D.C.

Platt hadn't seen his ex-wife in more than five years. She looked good but that was no surprise. Outer appearances had always been of utmost importance to her.

"You took back your maiden name?" The words fell out of his mouth before he could stop them.

"And my new husband agreed I should keep it."

Her smile was tight, framed with tiny new crinkles, but Platt was struck by how familiar her gestures still were to him. And how much she reminded him of Ali. It was hard to believe five years had passed.

"You're married?" He had purposely lost track of her after their divorce. Anger overrode his curiosity.

"Yes." The answer was curt and meant to bring the discussion to an immediate end. She didn't ask about him. Instead she pointed to the chairs around the long table. "Make yourselves comfortable. Undersecretary Baldwin—"

"I'm Irene Baldwin," her boss said, coming into the room. "Thanks for joining us."

The older woman shook hands with the ease and charm of a successful CEO. Or, Platt couldn't help thinking, a slick politician. Baldwin wore her hair swept up. Her suit was probably an expensive designer model, simple and charcoal. She didn't bother with heels and was much shorter than Mary Ellen but no one would immediately notice. The woman carried herself with grace and authority. Her presence filled the room and she automatically took command. In minutes she had Roger Bix giving a long, drawn-out account of both school contaminations as well as sharing his personal insights.

However, Bix was good, too. And Platt was impressed. The account Bix gave—although sounding complete and including what Platt began to realize halfway through the telling was insignificant nonsense—left out pertinent information and vital details. In other words, Bix was only pretending to share.

"We'll help in any way possible," Baldwin told them.

"I'm glad to hear that. A notification to all schools in the surrounding districts would be a good start."

"That's not possible," Mary Ellen said, garnering a scowl from her boss. But she didn't seem to notice, or perhaps she didn't care. "How can we notify schools when we don't even know what's making these children sick?"

"We'll know by tomorrow morning," Platt said in such a convincing tone that even Bix stared at him. They had to figure it out. Come Monday afternoon more kids would be getting sick somewhere.

"Still so sure of yourself." His ex-wife gave him another one of those tight smiles that seemed to say, *I know you better than that.*

"If we can tell you what made them sick, can you track down the supplier?" Bix asked Irene Baldwin, wisely ignoring the sideshow taking place across the table.

"Of course," Baldwin told him.

But Platt saw on Mary Ellen's face that Baldwin's promise might not be possible.

"You'll give us full access to the records? No proprietary stuff blackened out?"

"We'll track down the offending supplier together, if it indeed turns out to be a supplier. Food safety is the priority."

"I'm glad to hear that, because the last time I worked with this department they seemed hesitant to disclose and even more hesitant to punish one of their longtime suppliers."

Silence.

Bix wiped at an imaginary speck on the table in front of him. Knowing Bix, it was another way of telling Baldwin she wouldn't be able to fool him. That he could spot even the tiniest imperfections.

"I won't bother asking about the last time you worked with this department," Baldwin finally said. "That would mean defending procedures that I knew nothing about."

"It's been my experience that the USDA is sometimes ... not always"—he held up his hands as if in mock surrender—"but sometimes, has been slow to take our lead. What's that old axiom? The federal government won't act till the bodies stack." Bix exaggerated his Southern drawl, maybe to sound more charming, but Platt saw Mary Ellen stare darts at him. Baldwin, however, appeared unfazed.

"I can assure you that will not be the case under my watch. Now, if we're finished for the day, I promised Ms. Wychulis that I wouldn't keep her all night from her doting husband and new baby."

Baldwin stood up and everyone followed suit except Platt, who thought his knees would buckle in if he tried.

"You have a baby?" he asked.

"Yes, a son."

"I'm sorry," Baldwin interjected. "Do you two know each other?"

"Colonel Platt used to be my husband," Mary Ellen explained. To Platt she added, "I've moved on."

And she did, making her way with the others toward the door.

Platt trailed behind. His ears filled with the hiss of a wind tunnel and the thump-thump of his heart. Everyone walked in slow motion. Lips moved but made no sound. More smiles. A glance back at him. His chest ached. His breath felt obstructed. He silently gulped in air through his mouth.

"Platt, are you coming?" Julia waited at the door.

Bix and the women had already gone out into the hall-way.

Platt nodded and made his feet obey, but a voice in the back of his head kept repeating, "You haven't moved on. You haven't even begun to move on."

THIRTY-EIGHT

Maggie thought Wesley Stotter's tale, though interesting, sounded too fantastic to be true. She hoped she might get some answers out of Dawson. She left Donny to figure out what to do with the entertaining Stotter.

On her way out of the cafeteria she went through the line again and grabbed a piece of chocolate cake for Dawson.

She was glad to see him awake until she got a good look at his eyes.

"He's here," he whispered instead of a greeting. His head jerked back and forth as if he expected someone to jump out of the room's dark corners.

"Who are you talking about?"

She set the piece of cake on the cart beside him. He looked past it. Looked past her, over her shoulder, trying to see out the door.

"I saw him walk by the door three times."

She stayed in his line of vision, shifting and trying to get him to meet her eyes. He was panicked, sweat glistening on his face, his arms pushing himself up.

"I know he was in here. I could smell him."

She wondered if it was a reaction to the drugs they were giving him for pain. Or maybe it was simply the aftereffect of the electrical shock. She knew disorientation and incoherency could linger. So could the blurred vision.

"What does he smell like?"

"River mud. And sweat."

She turned on a lamp in the corner of the room and came back to stand close to him.

"You think he wants to hurt you?"

"He said I'd be sorry." His eyes flittered by, touching her face briefly before going off again. "Said I'd be sorry I survived."

She wished she had talked to Lucy about side effects of salvia. Could the hallucinations return? Certainly the hospital staff had done a toxicology workup on Dawson. She needed to tell them about the salvia. Would this be another costly mistake?

"Dawson, you need to talk to me. I want to help you, but you have to let me in on what happened last night."

"Can't. I promised Johnny." He caught the slip and looked to see if she had caught it, too.

"Johnny's dead, Dawson."

He stared at her as if waiting for a punch line.

"Johnny's not dead. I saw him this morning."

"He was here?"

"Yeah. You mean Kyle and Trevor. I know they're dead."

"Yes. And so is Johnny. We found him this afternoon." She paused to let it sink in. "He may have taken an overdose of something."

She was silent, not sure what to expect. What did teenagers do when they found out a friend was dead? Dawson was already imagining a stranger who smelled of river mud.

"What about Amanda?" His eyes were still worried.

"Was Amanda Johnny's girlfriend?"

He frowned as if he had to think about it. His mind was probably still fuzzy. Then he said, "Yeah, I guess so."

"She's fine." Maggie watched for his reaction to see if he had a crush on Amanda.

His eyes darted to the door, slid to Maggie's face, and jerked to the door again. Then he laid back.

"I can't believe Johnny's dead."

To Maggie's surprise the news about his friend's death appeared to calm him, but just a little. He settled into the pillows. Ran his free hand through his hair. His other hand still had an IV needle connecting him to a bag of solution. His eyes settled down.

"Is your mom or dad here with you?" Maggie glanced around the room. There were no jackets or magazines. No purse or tote bag. No abandoned coffee cups or soda cans.

"My dad'll stop by after work."

"And your mom?"

"My mom hasn't been around for a long time." He said this as a matter of fact, without sadness or anger.

"I'm sorry," Maggie said automatically then wanted to kick herself. She hated when people asked about her father, especially after she told them he was killed when she was twelve. "Lame response," she told Dawson. "But I am sorry you're alone."

He noticed the cake and looked up at her. "Is this for me?"

"Yes. I brought it up from the cafeteria."

He grabbed the plate and fork and started shoving in bites, suddenly looking much more like a normal teenager.

"You're not from around here."

"It's that obvious?"

He just shrugged. Kept on eating. She saw him glance inside her jacket where he could see her shoulder holster and weapon.

Maggie ventured closer.

"Dawson, you need to tell me what happened last night. Because I'm having an awful time trying to figure it all out."

His eyes darted back to the doorway.

"I promise you won't get in trouble." Even as she said this she sensed his panic. "But I can't protect you if I don't know what to protect you from."

He finished the cake. Left the plate on his tray and took

a long draw at the straw in his water glass. He was studying her, trying to decide whether or not to trust her.

"I know about the salvia," she said and saw his eyes
widen. "I don't care who brought it or where you got it. I
just need to know what happened. What were you doing in
the forest?"

"My dad was a quarterback in high school."

Maggie had no idea what this had to do with anything.
Would he just avoid all her questions? Still, she listened.

"He really liked Johnny." Dawson stared at his hands,
twisted the top of the bedsheets. "Sometimes I think he
wished Johnny was his son instead of me."

He paused. He was waiting for her to say something.
Another one of those knee-jerk responses like "I'm sorry."
She stayed quiet. She had no idea what to say to that.

"I just wanted to fit in. You know, be cool." He looked up
to make sure she was listening. "I was just excited they
invited me."

"Last night wasn't the first time?"

"Third, for me."

"It was an invitation-only party?"

"For some. Some new kids were always invited. Kind of
a test."

"Like an initiation?"

He shrugged.

"You always tried different drugs?"

He shrugged again.

"You're not going to get in trouble," she reassured him.

"I'm just trying to figure out what happened."

But she could see he was still trying to decide what to tell her and what to leave out.

"Were you filming your experiences for YouTube?"

His eyes flashed and she knew she'd hit on a kernel of truth.

"You found the camera." Not a question but an admission.

She didn't admit that they had not. Why didn't they find one? Had someone taken it before they arrived at the scene?

"And what about the pig's blood," she tried another shot in the dark.

To this he just shook his head.

"That was some dumb-ass idea of Johnny's. He wanted to see what the losers would do if he splattered them with blood."

She noticed he was still holding the fork she had brought with the piece of cake. He waggled it in one hand then shifted to the other, back and forth.

"Who attacked you, Dawson? Was that part of the ritual?"

"No. Absolutely not."

"Who was it then?"

"I don't know." And the panic returned.

"I need your help, Dawson."

For the first time he really looked at her. He was scared, but also perplexed that someone would ask such a thing of him.

"You need *my* help?"

"Yes. Will you help me?"

He almost smiled but then the teenager in him took control and he pretended to be negotiating when he said, "If you get me another piece of that cake I'll tell you whatever you want."

THIRTY-NINE

—————

The nurses' station was empty when Maggie came back with two plates of chocolate cake. She had forgotten a fork for herself and instead of making another trip down to the cafeteria she hoped the nurses might have a plastic one. But no one was in sight.

As she approached Dawson's room down the hallway she could see that the light she had left on in the room had been turned out. There was only the red-and-green glow from the monitors. Maybe she was breaking hospital rules, hanging around after lights-out.

From a few feet outside the door, she could see there was someone inside the room, bent over Dawson's bed. A man. His broad back to the doorway. Maybe Dawson's dad. She turned to leave them. She'd let them have their privacy. Dawson said his dad would come by after he got off work.

Then Maggie took another look. Something wasn't right.

She squinted, trying to adjust her eyes from the bright hallway to the dark room. The man held a pillow in one hand. He was adjusting Dawson's pillows. She started to turn away again.

Stopped again. This time she could see Dawson's fingers gripping the man's arm.

"Hey," she yelled and raced through the doorway.

Both of her hands were filled with plates. The man turned and bolted right at her, head down like a football player. He shoved his elbow up, catching her in the chest. The plates dropped and shattered. Maggie fell hard against one of the monitors and set it beeping. She scrambled to her feet, automatically drawing her weapon.

"Dawson?" She punched the instrument panel above his bed until a blue light flickered on and the Call button was activated.

Dawson was sitting up, holding his neck. Coughing.

"Are you okay?" She was half out of the room, looking up and down the hallway. A door banged under the far exit sign. "Are you okay?"

His eyes were wide but he gave her a thumbs-up.

She almost knocked a nurse over as she dashed out.

"What's going on?"

"Call the police," she managed to yell as her hip slammed against the door latch.

She stopped in the stairwell. Let the door thump shut.

Then she listened. Had he gone up or down?

She didn't hear any footsteps. Could he have already

exited on one of the other levels? She had to be only steps behind him.

She held her breath. Tried to slow her pulse. Listened again.

Nothing. Damn!

He must have already left the stairwell. She grabbed the door handle, ready to go back. It was locked. Of course, it was locked. All the levels would be. Standard security. You could leave but not reenter. Which meant he would need to go all the way down to the exit. Probably out into the parking lot.

Which meant he was still in the stairwell. Waiting for her.

FORTY

The dim lights in the stairwell cast more shadows than light. Maggie stayed pressed against the cinder-block wall as she slipped down one step then another. She kept her Smith and Wesson nose-down, both hands steadying her grip, trigger finger ready. She had no idea if the man in Dawson's room had a weapon. Just because he chose a pillow to smother Dawson didn't mean he wasn't carrying something more lethal.

She couldn't see beyond the next landing and she didn't dare hang over the railing to get a good look. No better way to get your head blown off. She slithered all the way down to the next set of stairs and peeked at the landing below.

Nothing. And still no sound.

Maybe he had already made it down to the ground floor. He could have exited and kept the door from slamming on his way out. As quietly as possible, she slipped out of her leather jacket, keeping crinkles and wisps to a minimum.

She loved this jacket, worn and comfortable, the two of them had been through a lot together. She rolled it up, lining on the outside, just like her mother had taught her. Without leaning forward she tossed it.

There was a shuffle of shoes on concrete then a whoosh. Maggie looked down in time to see the man withdrawing his hand and the gleam of a knife blade from his jacket.

"Stop. FBI."

He turned and was gone, banging his way down the steps.

She followed. Her heart thumped in her ears now. Sweat trickled down her back. It sounded like he was taking the steps two at a time. She tried quickening her pace. Only one more flight and he'd reach the exit.

She caught a glimpse of a black jacket. Maybe a stocking cap? It sounded like work boots, something heavy, but no clicking heel.

A door slammed. He was out.

Maggie raced down to the exit and almost elbowed it open, not wanting to give him another step ahead. But she stopped herself again. If he had waited for her on the landing what would stop him from waiting for a second shot at her on the other side of this door.

Damn!

She tried to settle her breathing, slow down her heartbeat. Neither cooperated. She could smell wet dirt or some kind of sludge. What was it that Dawson had said? The man smelled of river mud. She looked down at the concrete. He'd left dirt crumbles and footprints.

Yes, he'd screwed up.

Footprints were almost as good as leaving his fingerprints. But no time to celebrate. She blew her hair out of her eyes. Not relinquishing, she kept her two-handed grip on her weapon.

The door latch was a typical bar across the middle. Pushing anywhere on it unlatched the door. He had a knife. He now knew that she had a gun. He'd have to jump at her, which meant he'd have to hide behind the door when it opened.

She backed up a few steps. Steadied her grip on the gun. Sucked in a long breath. Then she kicked the bar as hard as she could, sending the door flying so that it slammed on the outside wall. Anyone hiding there would now have a broken nose or broken wrist if he was holding out a knife. But the door hit the outside wall. No one in between.

Maggie stepped outside into the dark. None of the lights from the parking lot's pole lamps hit this corner. She scanned the side of the building in case the man was pressed up against it, hiding in the shadows. There was no movement. A car drove by on the street but the engine wasn't revved, the tires weren't peeling out.

She got down on her hands and knees where she could see underneath the rows of vehicles. No feet. There was no Dumpster to hide behind. No air-conditioning system.

Where the hell did he go?

Then it occurred to her. Had he gotten into one of the vehicles? Of course, he'd have one waiting. Somewhere in this dark parking lot was he sitting in his vehicle, slouched down into the shadows and watching her?

She stayed alongside the building, her weapon was still clutched in her hand down by her side as she walked around to the front entrance of the hospital.

She heard a train in the distance. No sirens yet. She pulled out her cell phone. Thumbed her way through Contacts until she found Donny's number. She might not be able to search every vehicle in the parking lot, but she could find out whether or not that footprint matched the one taken from the forest.

It could be a break for them, but at the same time she realized any hope she'd had of Dawson Hayes helping was probably gone now.

FORTY-ONE

It was late by the time Julia came home, or rather by the
time she got to Rachel's town house. The place still didn't
feel like home, although she'd never admit that out loud, as
much to protect herself as Rachel. Home wasn't a place. It
was a state of mind and for some reason she hadn't wrapped
her mind around being a part of this household. But it was
tough. Rachel and CariAnne had been on their own, just the
two of them, for a very long time.

Julia heard the TV in the family room and thought Rachel
would be watching the news. She couldn't stay away from
it, checking the headlines on her smartphone every half
hour, sometimes more often if something big was happening. This was probably an every-fifteen-minutes day. So she
was surprised to find CariAnne in the oversized recliner, her
little body wrapped in a bright yellow blanket and swal-
lowed by the big chair.

"What are you doing still up?"

"Watching Leno."

She said it like it was something she did every night. Did she even know who Jay Leno was?

"How are you feeling?" Julia sat on the sofa, a safe two feet away.

"Still kinda yucky. But better."

"Is that popcorn I smell?"

"It sounded good."

"Your mom's letting you have popcorn?"

"Just a little."

"And she's letting you stay up late?"

"I slept like forever when I got home. I'm wide awake now."

"Ah, you're just in time," Rachel said, bringing in a tray.

Julia noticed there were three bowls of popcorn and three cans of cold soda. That was the stuff that tripped up her heart—being included so automatically.

"We're watching Leno."

"I heard. I didn't realize you knew there were other channels that didn't have twenty-four-hour news."

CariAnne giggled. She pulled the remote from under the yellow blanket.

"You rule!" Julia said and put up her hand for the girl to high-five her. "I'm glad you're feeling better, kiddo."

"Me, too."

"So what made the kids sick? Do they know?"

"Not yet." Julia grabbed a handful of popcorn. She hoped Rachel wouldn't probe further.

"Did anybody die?"

"CariAnne!"

"I'm just asking."

"I don't think anybody's dead." Julia smiled at Rachel's horror, realizing her precious little girl would dare to be as blunt as her mother.

It still surprised Julia to see Rachel, the mom. The woman reported some of the most gruesome crimes in the District. In fact, they liked to tell people how they had met over the dead bodies of a hooker and her pimp. Rachel definitely wasn't naïve or a newcomer when it came to the brutalities that people were capable of. But when it came to her daughter, Rachel was upset by the slightest sign that CariAnne was aware of the ugly facts.

Julia, of course, had learned how to be a grown-up when she was ten. She thought kids were coddled too much as it was.

"My friend Lisa gets to spend the night in the hospital," CariAnne told Julia and exchanged a look with her mom.

"Lisa's very sick," Rachel said. "I keep telling CariAnne that staying overnight at the hospital is not like a slumber party."

"Yeah, she probably has to have needles stuck in her arm."

"Julia!"

"Ewww. I hate needles."

"Twelve kids were hospitalized," Rachel told Julia. "They

said the CDC and Homeland Security were at the school. Is that true?"

By now Julia thought that was probably old news. So without hesitation she answered, "Yes."

A news alert flashed at the bottom of the television screen. The block type crawled across the bottom telling about the District public-school outbreak and said that it was caused by a negligent food handler.

"That's not true," Julia said. "Who the hell are they getting their information from?"

The last part of the statement moved across the screen.

" . . . according to the Secretary of Agriculture."

FORTY-TWO

———

After dropping off Julia and Bix, Platt had driven directly to USAMRIID. He had left Digger with his parents so going home to an empty house didn't even entice him. The little dog would act as a better security alert than their electronic system. Before he left, Platt had told his father about the black SUV that had tailed him from the diner.

"Just be careful," he had warned his dad.

"Always am" was the response, but Platt knew his parents lived in a whole other world. And he hated that he may have brought one of the dangers from his life into theirs.

He had called them several times throughout the day and everything appeared to be normal. He was hoping last night's incident was more curiosity than threat.

For the last hour he had kept himself so busy that he didn't think about Ali, Mary Ellen, or the miserable memories that had flooded his head. He concentrated on preparing slides from the garbage he and Racine had bagged along with some of the vomit. Bix had even shared some samples from the sick high schoolers in Norfolk. It hadn't taken long before he found the bacterium—salmonella. But Bix was right. It was an unusual strain.

By now the scientists down in Atlanta knew what they were dealing with. Usually the bacterium was found in ground beef, poultry, or eggs. Sometimes it even ended up on raw vegetables or fruit. Platt also knew that some strains had become resistant to the antibiotics that were fed to cattle and poultry.

Confirming what the bacterium was didn't make it any easier to decipher what food it had hidden in. Platt was hoping that's where his samplings of the schoolkids' vomit would come in handy as well as the food packaging.

Under the microscope the bacteria looked like tiny pegs jammed in among the cells. They attached themselves to the linings of the gastrointestinal organs. The bacteria would work their way through the stomach, inflaming the mucosa and usually causing severe vomiting. From there the bacteria continued migrating down, depositing themselves onto the walls of the intestine, causing it to bloat and dilate. That's what caused the extreme pain and diarrhea. If the pesky critters decided to take an additional stay in the colon during their trip down, they could force the inner lining to tear away. The entire passage took less than two hours.

Less-severe cases were often misdiagnosed as stomach flu or irritable bowel syndrome. Truth was, sudden bouts of stomach flu didn't happen that often. Most people didn't realize that their upset stomach—especially within two to six hours after a meal—was mostly caused by some food-borne bacteria.

Ali had the stomach flu. That was all that Mary Ellen thought it was. It was her reason, her explanation for not calling Platt, for not telling him sooner. He had been in Afghanistan just after the start of the war, a world away, but he would have commandeered the fastest ride home if he had known his daughter was seriously ill. He had never been able to forgive Mary Ellen for waiting to contact him. She had waited too long and he had never had a chance to even say good-bye to his little girl.

Seeing Mary Ellen today and hearing that she had a new husband and a new baby should have reminded that him what had happened in the past was an awfully long time ago. Instead the memories, the physical pain was still so close to the surface. He felt as though she had ripped a scab off a wound—a wound that had never healed properly.

He sat back from the microscope. Rubbed his face, hoping to wipe away the exhaustion. He plucked through his assortment of "leftovers" and "Dumpster" samples, wondering where to begin, when his cell phone rang. He almost shoved it away until he noticed the caller ID, then he couldn't grab it fast enough.

He caught his breath before he answered, "Hey, Maggie O'Dell."

"I keep forgetting you're an hour ahead of me. Did I wake you?"

"No, I'm still at the lab."

"At USAMRIID?"

"Yeah, a weird case. I'm trying to help the CDC figure out what made a hundred and five schoolkids sick."

"Food poisoning?"

"Looks like it. I'm pretty certain it's a salmonella strain but it hit two different schools in the same week. About two hundred miles apart. I'm surprised you haven't heard about it. It's all over the news."

"Actually I haven't seen or heard the news since yesterday. Been a little weird here, too."

"Sure, conferences can be that way."

"I'm not at the conference."

"Oh." He wanted to kick himself because his immediate response was that he was hurt she hadn't told him. "Are you okay?"

"I'm okay. Just a little ... overwhelmed," she said.

Platt knew it was a lot for her to admit. They had started out as doctor and patient and sometimes Platt too easily reverted to that role. He couldn't help it. He cared about her, more than he was willing to admit—at least, to her. It was only recently that he had admitted it to himself. He couldn't risk losing her as a friend.

Platt knew Maggie was skittish when it came to romantic entanglements. That's what she called them: "entanglements." Amazing what could be learned about a person's attitude toward something just by listening to the words she used to describe it. She didn't talk about her divorce except to say how exhausting the marriage had been. And she didn't talk about past entanglements, either.

To be fair, he hadn't told her much about his marriage. There were large chunks of their lives that they hadn't shared. Maybe they didn't know each other as well as he thought. He did know that Maggie wouldn't let anyone take care of her. And she rarely let down her guard. It was a big deal for her to even admit that she was overwhelmed.

"Tell me what's going on," he said.

She gave him an abbreviated rundown, which made him tense. Once again, she was chasing a killer. Coming way too close for his comfort level. No matter how many times he told himself it was what she did for a living, it still set him on edge.

"You're right about the laser stun gun," Platt said. "The military's had the technology for a long time but it's only recently they've managed to funnel its power into a small-enough weapon. From what I remember it's the size of a rifle, and I think you still have to carry a backpack with some sort of charger. Originally it was developed for crowd control. All you have to do is sweep an area with the laser beam. You don't have to connect like a stun gun or shoot an attached dart like a Taser. But from what I understand, it's not meant to kill anyone."

"Is it possible the military would stage war games in the middle of a Nebraska forest?"

"Actually it sounds like the perfect place. But they wouldn't use a bunch of drugged teenagers for targets."

"Are you sure about that?"

Platt took a deep breath to keep from getting defensive. He knew Maggie was simply looking at all angles but he tended to get his back up when anyone attacked the military. Sure, mistakes were made. And he had witnessed firsthand the corruption and abuse of power. He had exposed a couple of incidents himself. But he still wanted to believe they were rare.

"Right now," she said, "it seems my options are GIs gone wild or red-eyed aliens."

He laughed and finally she did, too.

Then completely out of nowhere, he blurted, "I miss you."

Her silence made his stomach clench but for the first time, he realized he didn't care.

"Okay, what's wrong?" she asked.

"What? I can't tell you I miss you without something being wrong?"

"I can hear it in your voice. Something's going on."

"It's just . . . do you ever think you'll want to have kids?" As soon as he said it, he knew he had stepped over the line.

"Ben, I don't even know yet whether you wear boxers or briefs and you're asking me if I want to have kids?"

He laughed again. Felt some of the tension drain away. He imagined her on the other end. She'd be smiling but shaking her head at him. Probably pacing. He knew she couldn't stand still when she talked on the phone. If he was really making her nervous she'd be pushing a strand of hair back behind her ear right about now. The one thing he took away from her comment was that she used the word "yet." She didn't know "*yet*" if he wore boxers or briefs. One word could reveal a lot.

"Are you okay?" she asked after a long silence.

"Yeah, I'm okay. This case is probably just getting to me," he lied.

"You're thinking about Ali," she said and it wasn't a question.

Maybe they actually knew each other too well.

FORTY-THREE

NEBRASKA

Lucy had left the light on for Maggie. The scent of freshly brewed tea and cinnamon filled the kitchen.

When she'd called Lucy earlier, Maggie had suggested she stay in North Platte, find a hotel room. Her suitcase was, after all, in the trunk of the rented Toyota. And she didn't want to wear out her welcome. Lucy had been kind enough to take her in last night when they were all too exhausted to think clearly, but she certainly didn't expect the woman to extend her invitation.

"It does take a bit longer to drive out here," Lucy had said. "I'll certainly understand if you'd rather stay in town, but I also would enjoy the company." As if needing to reaffirm that she wasn't simply being polite, she added, "I just put a batch of homemade cinnamon rolls in the oven."

Now Maggie found the woman reading in the living

room, a small fire crackling in the brick fireplace. The group of dogs huddled around Lucy all got up at once and came to Maggie, wagging and demanding attention, butting each other playfully out of the way.

Maggie sank down into the recliner opposite Lucy and petted each dog. She had never had her own mother wait up for her. Instead, Maggie—even as a twelve-year-old—was the one waiting up for her mother, who sometimes didn't come home at all. Now suddenly she was struck by how good this place felt—warm, cozy, and safe. Not even twenty-four hours and it felt like home.

Lucy looked up at her over half-moon reading glasses and set her book aside.

"You look exhausted," she said. "How are you?"

"Exhausted." Maggie smiled. "But I'm okay." Jake pushed his snout under her hand, asking to be petted and she automatically obeyed. The others had settled by Lucy's feet again.

"Someone takes care of your dog while you're away?"

"Yes."

"Someone who takes care of you, too, when you're there?"

"Oh, no." She shook her head and was immediately embarrassed that she had protested so quickly. At the same time she didn't want to explain that her FBI partner, R. J. Tully—who was taking care of Harvey—was very much involved with her best friend, Gwen Patterson.

"But there is someone? Someone new in your life?"

Maggie stared at the woman, wondering how she seemed to have the power to look deep beneath the surface.

"Maybe," Maggie said, still thinking about her conversation with Platt, how good it was to hear his voice. She loved the sound of his laughter. Just sharing with him the events of the last twenty-four hours had made her feel less alone in the world. "Trouble is I've gotten used to being on my own. I like scheduling my time without getting someone else's approval."

In her mind she added that being alone meant being safe. No one could hurt or disappoint you if you didn't let them get close. The fact that she missed Benjamin Platt annoyed her. It felt like a weakness, a vulnerability. "Is that being independent," she asked, "or selfish?"

"There always has to be a balance. It should never be all or nothing." Lucy hesitated, deciding whether or not to go on. "You should never deny who you are to please someone else. If that's the choice, then it's not meant to be.

"My mother was full-blooded Omaha. She did everything she possibly could to deny it, to leave it behind. I think that's why she married my father. He was the son of Irish Catholic immigrants. A railroad engineer who had dreams as big as a Nebraska sky. But he absolutely adored American history and the Indian culture. He was the one who taught me about the Omaha tribe and my Indian heritage. I think my mother finally learned to love it, through his eyes.

"Your independence, your time alone, when you find

someone who loves those things as much as you do and wants them for you, you'll find that those things no longer matter unless you also have that particular person beside you. A bit ironic, I suppose."

Lucy didn't push the matter. Instead she asked, "How's the boy doing?"

Maggie had told her on the phone about the intruder and the attempt on Dawson's life.

"He's scared. But his dad's with him and Skylar has a deputy outside his door now. Donny seems certain the stranger's footprint is going to match the one we found in the forest. It has the same distinctive waffle pattern. Same size."

"Even if it matches, it might not lead us anywhere. There must be hundreds of pairs of work boots in this area. Did Dawson tell you anything?"

Maggie shook her head. "Not really. They used the campsite to experiment with drugs. He did admit they had a camera."

"And we didn't find it. Could they have caught something on film?"

"I have no idea. What else is out there besides a bunch of trees and pasture?"

"The university has a new field house on one side and there's the nursery on the other side."

"Nursery?"

"The Forest Service grows their own trees. The forest doesn't replenish itself. Trees don't grow well in sand." She smiled, then realized that wasn't enough of an explanation. "It was an experiment at the turn of the last century— 1902, if I remember correctly. Every tree was hand planted. About twenty thousand acres. Originally it was believed that settlers would come to the area if they were provided an easy supply of timber to build with. It's been sort of an open-air laboratory ever since. When trees die, as many of those original pine are doing now, they have to be replenished."

"Doesn't sound very sinister."

Lucy laughed. "No, I'm afraid not."

"What's in the field house?"

"I'm not sure. The university built it several years ago. I think it was supposed to be a research laboratory for developing plant hybrids. I'm not a fan of genetic-engineering our food. But from what I heard they decided to use someplace else."

"So it's empty?"

"No. I believe the Department of Agriculture uses it for something. Not sure what. You can't see it from the road. Once in a while I've seen a vehicle coming out."

"You've never been curious?"

"It's a secured entry and fenced off."

"Electric fencing?"

Lucy took off her eyeglasses. "What exactly are you thinking?"

"Not sure. I don't remember seeing the facility when we were there. Can you see it from the kids' campsite?"

Lucy gave it some thought before answering. "I don't think so."

Maggie sighed, disappointed.

"However," Lucy added, her long fingers massaging her right temple, "I think you might be able to see the private road that goes from the main route to the facility."

Maggie's cell phone rang in her jacket pocket. She jumped up to retrieve it realizing that she hoped it was Platt. He had caught her off guard earlier with his question about children. Recently she had almost convinced herself she wanted to take their relationship to the next level, but not if it meant embarking on an emotional mission to replace his beloved dead child.

She yanked the phone from her pocket. It wasn't Platt. She tried to keep her disappointment from Lucy. Too late. The woman didn't miss a thing.

"Investigator Fergussen, you must have some new information."

"Not anything good but I thought you'd want to know. Car accident. About an hour ago."

She could hear sirens and voices yelling. He must be on the site.

"Victims are Courtney Ressler and Nikki Everett. Looks like they were coming around a curve. Ran right into a six-point buck."

"A buck?"

"Deer. Probably didn't see it until it was too late. You know teenagers. Might have been going too fast. Texting."

"Are they okay?"

"Negative. Both were dead on impact. It's pretty messy. Just thought you'd like to know."

"Thanks."

Lucy hadn't taken her eyes off Maggie but waited patiently.

"We just lost two more teenagers from last night."

SATURDAY, OCTOBER 10

FORTY-FOUR

___

WASHINGTON, D.C.

Platt felt like he'd only been asleep for a few minutes when Bix's phone call dragged him back out of bed.

"United ticket counter. Reagan National. Meet me there at five thirty. We've got a six thirty flight."

"I'm hoping you mean five thirty this afternoon," Platt had said looking at his bedside alarm clock that read three forty-five.

"Very funny. I'll see you there."

Now seated in first class beside the CDC chief, Platt was pleased to see that Bix looked even worse than he did. Bix's hair was tousled and his eyes were bloodshot. But Roger Bix in a suit and necktie was serious business even if the tie hung loose. The jacket had come off as soon as they stepped onto the plane and was sent away with a flight attendant while Bix rolled up his shirtsleeves and shoved them above his elbows. Platt wore his uniform as instructed, but he had sur-rendered his jacket to the flight attendant, too.

It wasn't until they were in the air that Bix started to explain why they were making an early-morning flight to Chicago.

"I think our friend"—*friend* being their code word for the anonymous caller—"got pissed by the USDA's announce-ment last night."

"What announcement?"

"You didn't hear the news?"

"I went to USAMRIID then home."

"The secretary of agriculture himself said that the school contamination was caused by a negligent kitchen worker who was being suspended."

Platt thought about poor Velma Carter. "How did they come up with that? We didn't even mention the woman at our meeting."

"Exactly why our friend is pissed. So he's given us a bigger piece of the puzzle."

"In Chicago?"

"A processing plant on the north side. They get scraps and chunks of beef from various slaughterhouses, combine them, then grind them up. They take the ground beef and make it into patties, meatballs, spice it up for tacos."

"Let me guess, those get shipped off to schools."

"If only it was that simple." He pulled out a thick file from his briefcase. "I've been trying to make heads or tails out of this mess."

"You're assuming it was the beef in the taquito that was contaminated?"

"Not assuming."

"Your guys found something?"

"I can't frickin' sit around until you lab nerds finish studying your crap and vomit slides. I pushed our anonymous caller. He was feeling slightly guilty. That ridiculous statement from the USDA pushed him to tell me where to look."

"He told you it was the beef?"

"Suggested. Not told. My lab nerds are checking it out this morning."

"So why do we need to go to Chicago?"

Bix shrugged. "Maybe this guy isn't really a whistleblower. Maybe he just wants to yank our chain. But I got the feeling giving us this tip was huge."

"So did you have time to check out this processing plant?"

"Family owned. Been in business for fifty years. I tried to pull up the inspection records at the USDA, and get this—I was told that information was only available by filing a request through the Freedom of Information Act because the records must contain 'proprietary information.'"

"Why don't they just black it out?"

"That's what they will do once we've filed our request."

"I thought Baldwin was going to make everything available?"

"That's what she said, didn't she? However, I couldn't

reach her this early in the morning. Got her voice-messaging service. Told her to fuckin' call me. We need an immediate notice to all schools about beef products and we need a recall."

"So?"

"Didn't hear from her before I had to switch off my phone."

"She seemed genuine last night. Give her a chance to do the right thing."

"I am. But she has less than forty-eight hours."

FORTY-FIVE

Mary Ellen hated leaving her husband and son fast asleep. She had barely gotten to see the two of them last night before bedtime. And now, on a Saturday morning, she was back outside the conference room, all props sorted and collated, coffee and Danish laid out. Everyone was here, except for Irene Baldwin. Once again, she was keeping them all waiting for an emergency meeting she had called.

Mary Ellen felt on edge. It didn't help matters that she had allowed herself three coffees already this morning. Her stomach burned and her nerves were stripped raw. She wanted to be angry at Benjamin Platt and yet all she could think about was how good the bastard looked. She should, at least, take pleasure in his obvious misery when he discovered that she was married and had moved on.

Last night, lying in bed she told herself that she was the luckiest woman in the world. She had been given a second chance at having a family. When she closed her eyes she was shocked that all she could think about was Benjamin Platt and remember so vividly what it felt like to have him make love to her. She rolled over and cuddled into her husband's back, pressed her cheek against his shoulders, and begged for sleep.

"Wychulis."

Baldwin's heels clicked up the hallway. She looked like a woman who had slept eight hours and, unlike Mary Ellen, didn't need three cups of coffee this morning to get her moving. But on closer inspection Mary Ellen saw that her boss's attempt at concealing the bags under her eyes had not been totally successful.

"Have you heard from the secretary?"

"No."

"Of course not. He makes a ridiculous statement, and we're supposed to deal with the fallout."

Mary Ellen remained quiet. She knew her old boss must have had the necessary evidence before releasing his statement to the press.

"Are we ready here?"

"Yes."

Baldwin opened the door to the conference room and stopped. She stayed in the doorway and Mary Ellen almost bumped into her.

"Good morning, everyone. Thanks for coming. We'll be right with you."

Then Baldwin closed the door again and waved for Mary Ellen to follow her down the hallway.

"Who the hell are all those people?" she whispered.

"You asked to convene the Recall Committee. These are all standing members."

"There must be a dozen people in that room."

"Actually fourteen. Joseph Murray brought two of his techs and Karena McFerris has her deputy field inspection manager with her. What exactly are we going to talk about recalling?"

"Ground beef that the USDA bought specifically for the school lunch program."

"You do understand we won't be able to actually order it. All meat recalls are voluntary. We negotiate with the supplier."

Obviously Baldwin did not know because the look she gave Mary Ellen was one of disbelief.

"You're telling me the FDA can order a recall on a defective toy that might hurt children but the USDA cannot order a recall on contaminated meat that could kill children?"

Mary Ellen controlled her frustration.

"Our agency is to assist producers as well as protect consumers." She shouldn't need to remind Irene Baldwin that the reason she was hired over more qualified candidates—including Mary Ellen—was for her ability to bridge that gap.

"Is Undersecretary Eisler at least here?" Baldwin finally asked.

"He sent Deputy Administrator Jerold from Marketing

Service. Jerold is actually the person directly responsible for overseeing the National School Lunch Program."

Mary Ellen had never seen Baldwin like this. Since day one, the woman had appeared infallible. Mary Ellen wondered what her old boss, who hired Baldwin, would say if he could see the ex-CEO now.

FORTY-SIX

———

NEBRASKA

Maggie had forgotten about Johnny Bosh's cell phone. When she unpacked her suitcase to dress for another day of puzzle solving in the Sandhills, she found it buried in her dirty, musty-smelling clothes. Immediately she was reminded of her claustrophobic crawl underneath the Boshes' house. She shook off the thought and plugged her universal adapter into his phone.

By the time she showered and had breakfast with Lucy, the phone had charged.

And suddenly she had access to Johnny Bosh's world. What she wanted to see most were the text messages from the minutes or hours before his death. Text messages didn't disappear unless the cell-phone user erased each one. And even then it was sometimes possible to retrieve them.

Johnny's mother had said that she had spoken to a couple of his friends, but they hadn't heard from or seen him. Since he had his phone with him, Maggie suspected he had talked to or was waiting to talk to someone. She was right. But she wasn't prepared for what she found.

Johnny B DAW'S OK.
Amanda: WHO CARES? HE'S A LOSER.
Amanda: THEY'RE ALL LOSERS.
Johnny B: THEY'LL KEEP THEIR MOUTHS SHUT.
Amanda: YEAH, JUST LIKE TAYLOR.
Johnny B: THAT WAS DIFFERENT.
Amanda: NOT SO DIFFERENT. THIS TIME WE R SO SCREWED.
Amanda: U R NOT EVER LEAVING THIS PLACE.
Johnny B: THAT'D MAKE U HAPPY.
Amanda: YEP. YOU'LL BE STUCK HERE WITH THE REST OF US.
Amanda: NO FOOTBALL. NO SCHOLARSHIP.
Amanda: LOSER, LOSER, LOSER!!!!!

There was nothing more for almost an hour. Then several more from Amanda, asking where he was then demanding he answer her.

He never did.

Maggie decided she'd pay another visit to the girl.

FORTY-SEVEN

CHICAGO

Platt figured there might not be such a thing as a surprise inspection. Even the rain beating down on the tin roof sounded like it was announcing their arrival. The state health inspector had met them at the front entrance, bringing with him the last several inspection reports. Bix exploded when he saw the blacked-out sections.

"It's proprietary information," Inspector Alfred said without apology. "I do as I'm instructed. Besides, I think it's just their recipe for the taco seasoning. No big deal."

"Really," Bix said. "What if it's something in that seasoning that's making kids sick?"

"I doubt it."

Platt grimaced at the man's foolish attempt to argue with Bix. He started flipping pages while the other two men established their territory. He noticed several warnings and citations, but they appeared to be minor infractions.

Finally they were ready to move on. The three of them stopped at security so Bix and Platt could present their credentials. They were issued badges and security key cards that would allow them access throughout the facility. A tech handed out several pairs of shoe covers, telling the guests to change each time they entered a new area. The covers would be available at each entrance.

Platt still wasn't sure what Bix expected to find. Worse, he didn't think Bix knew.

They started with the production lines. The first one shaped ground beef into patties. A supervisor explained the process, step by step. Alfred didn't appear to be listening and concentrated instead on making notes and conducting his own checks. Platt wandered away from the group to look through glass doors into other sections.

They were told that the shift would end in an hour and they would be able to observe the wash down and cleaning of the equipment. They could take samples of the cleaning chemicals and do their own "wipe down" to check for residue. But Platt wasn't interested. He was certain it wasn't chemicals or residue of chemicals that was making these kids sick.

He watched another production line where scraps and chunks of beef were fed into a huge grinder. The beef would supply the other production lines. Lots of raw meat. Lots of potential.

"Where does the beef come from?" Platt asked the supervisor when the group caught up.

"Various places."

"Not just Illinois?"

"Oh gosh, no. Colorado, Nebraska, Florida, California, and Illinois—just to name a few states. We get the scraps and chunks from slaughterhouses that aren't used for commercial cuts."

"USDA contracts with you for the school lunch program?"

"USDA contracts with us, but I don't know about the school lunch program. We don't really know where all our products end up. We ship to state warehouses or other processors who might repackage and put their brand name on it for retail sale. Some of the product is bought by hospitals. And yeah, some is sent to school distribution centers."

"You don't have records of where your products end up?" Bix asked.

"No, sir. We only have records of which state warehouses we ship to. Those warehouses would probably have records of where they shipped the products."

"What about the slaughterhouses?" Platt asked. "Do they provide you with test samples for bacteria or do you do your own testing?"

"They provide their test results but we pull routine samples after we grind the meat."

"What happens when you get a positive back?"

"We're supposed to shut the line. Clean everything. Pull another sample."

"Every time?" Bix asked.

"Yup, every time."

Platt was concerned that the supervisor had said "we're supposed to" rather than "we do." Grinding beef that might already be contaminated usually ended up spreading it. Taking random samplings was a crapshoot at best.

They moved on to another area, and again Platt ventured off on his own. He noticed two workers entering one of the security doors. As they changed their shoe covers Platt noticed the old covers looked wet. One of the men carried a clean plastic bucket that he took over to the grinding line and filled with ground beef.

Curious, Platt went to check if this particular door actually led to the outside, wondering why a worker would be allowed to bring in an unsterile container, but he saw through the glass window that the door didn't lead outside. It led to what looked like a small warehouse.

Platt used his key card to open the door. Bix saw him and hurried over, bringing the other two men with him.

"I was just curious," Platt said.

Without going into the room he saw what had made the shoe covers wet. A drain in the middle of the floor was filled with murky sludge that gave off a rancid smell.

"Oh yeah, it backs up sometimes when it rains," the supervisor explained. "We've talked about that before." He exchanged looks with Alfred like it was okay since they had talked about it. "George," he called to a worker sorting supplies on the back shelves. "Clean this up."

Platt watched as George complied, going to a stack of

plastic buckets exactly like the one Platt had seen taken inside the production area and filled with ground beef. George took one off the same stack to mop up the floor.

"Are those disposable?" Platt asked.

"Not to worry. We send them through a special rinse cycle."

"Plastic?" Platt said and looked over at Bix, who was already trying not to scream.

FORTY-EIGHT

Wesley Stotter had done his homework. It was something his fans expected. He knew almost everything there was to know about the Nebraska National Forest. He could list every type of tree and every species of bird. He knew the forest was ninety thousand acres—fifteen miles wide and eleven miles from north to south. Twenty thousand of those acres were covered by trees, the rest, rolling pasture land. He had visited the campgrounds, climbed the observation tower, and been inside the nursery. But he didn't have a clue what went on inside the field house between the Dismal River and the forest.

Ordinarily he wouldn't care. But when the sun came up after his sleepless night in his stranded Roadmaster with his Colt .45 cradled in his hands, the first thing he noticed was the sunlight hitting the tin roof below. Where his vehicle had stalled had given him a bird's-eye view of the field house.

Tucked between sand dunes with the Dismal River winding behind it and the forest ridge on the other side, the complex remained shielded from view of the main road. It was easy to forget it existed. No one took an interest in something they couldn't see.

Before Stotter knew whether or not his car would start, he found himself curious about the windowless metal building. There were fields fenced off alongside the river, planted with wheat, corn, and an assortment of big leafy plants, maybe different kinds of vegetables. On the other side of the building was a huge parking lot. The concrete square reminded Stotter of a helipad. It extended all the way to the building, where there was a set of double-wide doors tall enough to drive in a very large truck or, perhaps, a small plane.

Yesterday in the early-morning hours, Stotter's main concern had been if anyone had seen him. The crops looked well tended but probably weren't checked every day. He had calculated how long it would take to hike all the way down to the building on his arthritic knees and wondered if it would even be worth the trip. But when he twisted the key in the ignition, the old Buick had fired right up, leaving him to wonder if it really had stalled or if the night before had all been a figment of his imagination.

Now back on the ridge but not quite as high up as he had been the previous morning, he knew one thing for certain: no one would expect him or see him approach from up above, out of the trees and brush, instead of through the open pasture or the access road. So whatever clandestine activities—if there were any—would not be alerted by his presence.

Through binoculars he scanned the complex before starting his hike down. He didn't see any security cameras anywhere though he suspected the thin, almost invisible wire that ran above the barbed-wire fence was hot.

He brought his camera but left the wireless mic. No live cam today. The photos would need to be his documentation. If he found anything.

He kept thinking about the creature he had seen running through the forest. It appeared to be the same creature his father described that had fallen from the sky over Roswell. Maybe that's what the lights were; the lights that had exploded right before his eyes while he videotaped them for his fans. It had happened only moments before those teenagers thought they were attacked in the forest. Stotter had already heard their stories. They claimed to have seen a creature with beams of lights shooting out of its arms.

If there had been a creature like the one the teenagers saw and the one Stotter had seen, was it possible there were more? And if so, where had they gone? It couldn't have been far without someone seeing them, just like Stotter had seen the one running through the trees. He was convinced the field house might be some sort of base.

It all sounded crazy, but that's what the government had said about his father's story. To this day they still weren't able to explain the wreckage of that strange aircraft. Instead of explaining, the government hid away the evidence, not realizing that Stotter's father hadn't surrendered all of the film that documented the event. Wesley Stotter had kept his father's secret all these years, taking seriously his responsibility for the photos that no one else knew existed.

Maybe now was finally the time to make those photos public. Stotter hoped the ones he shot today would be equally exciting.

FORTY-NINE

Maggie booted up her laptop. The breeze was crisp but the sun kept her warm as she sat on the porch off the loft bedroom. She caught herself thinking this place would be the perfect retreat, a real vacation getaway some day in the future. Some day when her mind wasn't preoccupied with the murder. Could it be possible that Nikki's and Courtney's deaths had *not* been an accident? Did Johnny really commit suicide?

Amanda and Dawson were the only two left from Thursday night's party in the forest. Dawson still had an armed deputy outside his hospital room. Maggie had called Amanda's house earlier to make sure she was okay. Her mother assured Maggie that she wasn't letting her daughter out of her sight. She said the girl hadn't left her bedroom except for meals. And now after learning that two more of her friends were dead, Mrs. Griffin knew her daughter "must be just devastated." But she agreed to let Maggie talk to the girl if she didn't upset her.

Before Maggie left, she wanted to check on some things that had her mind racing.

Lucy had warned her that the wireless connection might take a few seconds longer than she expected. Maggie had already noticed that cell-phone reception in the Sandhills could be sporadic.

While she waited she sorted through a pile of crime-scene photos Donny had left for her. She found one of the bite mark on Amanda Vicks's arm. There was no doubt it was made by human teeth, not an animal's. But still, there was something about the angle and the location that bothered Maggie.

She sat back and stared out at the rolling red-and-gold grasses. She couldn't remember ever seeing a sky this deep a shade of blue. Nor could she recall being able to see for such a long distance without having a building obstruct her view.

She thought about Lucy Coy living here alone with her dogs. Most people might think it a lonely existence but Maggie understood it completely. Being alone didn't mean being lonely. In fact, Maggie realized long ago that she associated being alone with being safe. The concept had protected her through her childhood, through her marriage and her divorce, and continued to guide her personal life.

Then along came Benjamin Platt.

She liked being with him, just having him silently beside her. She had never known anyone—other than Gwen Patterson—with whom she could be herself and not apologize for the occupational hazards of her job, for her stubborn independence. Like with Gwen, Maggie knew she could depend on Ben if she needed him. He understood her fierce commitment to doing the right thing no matter what the consequence. To a certain degree, he was guilty of the same impulse.

He made her laugh. And got her sense of humor. In less than a year he had become a good friend. She trusted him. But lately she couldn't think about him without remembering the tingle from the one kiss they had shared. It was months ago and she still thought about it. Silly, really. She had probably deprived herself of such sensation for too long. It was easier going without than getting entangled in the baggage that usually came along with such encounters.

There had been a hurricane bearing down on them and that had intensified the moment. Or at least, that's what she told herself. But now they avoided each other. Well, not really avoided. They talked to each other every day. But their busy schedules hadn't allowed them to spend time together. Yes, too busy—that's also what she told herself.

She forced her mind back to the computer screen. She had a hunch about something and wanted to check it out before she talked to Amanda. It took a couple of different searches and then she found what she wanted. It wasn't what she expected.

FIFTY

The rain hadn't let up. If anything, Platt thought it was coming down harder. The car Bix had hired to drive them wasn't out front as instructed, only giving the CDC chief yet another reason to blow one of his last proverbial gaskets. They watched the health inspector doing a comical skip-dance to his vehicle, leaping puddles and using his briefcase for an umbrella. Yet neither Bix nor Platt smiled.

"Your friend played us for a couple of chumps," Platt said.

Bix beat his umbrella against the brick wall until it popped open.

"Frickin' wild-goose chase," he agreed. "Let's see if the son-of-a-bitch driver is around the corner."

He lifted the umbrella, inviting Platt to share.

"Why would he send us all the way here just to take a look at some sanitary infractions?"

Bix shrugged. He didn't have an answer, seemed a bit embarrassed that he didn't have an answer.

Around the corner they found a chain-link fence and a security hut. No car, no driver. Beyond the fence was another part of the processing plant. Or at least that's what the building looked like at first glance, with the same brick façade and an enclosed walkway that connected it to the main structure. What appeared different was the security. The guard in the small hut was armed. And he was dressed in a military uniform.

"What is this place?" Platt asked but he could already see that Bix was just as mystified.

Through the glass of the walkway they could see an armored truck pull out from behind the secured building. There was obviously a separate entrance for this part of the plant.

"Shall we see what's inside?" Platt asked as they stood in the rain.

"Yeah, right."

"They can call the plant supervisor to vouch for us."

"Something tells me that guy wouldn't carry much weight on this side of the plant."

"We have credentials from USAMRIID and the CDC. I'm in uniform."

"Can they court-martial us for something like this?"

"You're a civilian. Civilians can't be court-martialed."

Bix considered this. "Okay, let's see how far we get."

Within ten minutes they were inside. It didn't take much longer before both men realized *this* was what the anonymous caller had hoped they would see. The laboratories rivaled those that Platt worked in every day. He was impressed. And in an unsavory way they reminded him of USAMRIID—but the past, rather than the present.

Men and women in white lab coats worked behind digital microscopes and computer screens. The walls were lined with rows and rows of computer monitors. Platt and Bix were told that the labs were run by the Department of Agriculture, advancing hybrids and continuing research on genetically engineered foods. It made sense to Platt until they passed a room with a huge electron microscope and other highly advanced equipment that he recognized and had only seen in his own labs at USAMRIID.

The manager of the plant introduced himself as Philip Tegan. He said he was used to senior officials—their credentials had, indeed, impressed him—dropping in to take a look. In fact, he seemed oddly excited to meet Platt and said it was about time someone from USAMRIID visited.

When Platt nonchalantly asked, "Why is that?" Tegan, whose birdlike features—beady narrow eyes separated by a sharp hooked nose and finished with a wobbly chin—squawked out a laugh as if Platt were joking.

"Well, because of the amazing programs USAMRIID

pioneered back in the 1970s. You might say we're following in your footsteps."

"Really?"

Platt hid his surprise and ignored Bix's "What the fuck?" look of confusion. Instead, he focused on encouraging Tegan to share, but it seemed the man had wisely become silent.

FIFTY-ONE

Amanda's mother had prepared coffee and miniature pastries, treating Maggie's visit as if it were a social call. Maggie remembered Sheriff Skylar talking about the family's prominence, so she was not surprised to find Cynthia Griffin with full makeup, bright red lipstick, and unmovable hair on a Saturday afternoon. And despite the expensive running suit, the woman didn't look like she was accustomed to breaking a sweat let alone jogging.

"I told Amanda you're here," Mrs. Griffin said. "Griff's not here. I didn't tell him you were coming." She prattled on, what sounded like a nervous habit to fill silence. "He tries so hard to protect Amanda and me. He's been on full alert since Johnny's death. It's just awful about Johnny, isn't it? And now those girls. Just awful."

She was trying to lead Maggie into the living room and

directing her to take a seat. In front of the sofa a glass-topped coffee table displayed delicate coffee cups and matching dessert plates, tiny pink-and-purple flowers hand-painted on shiny white china.

Maggie didn't follow. She stayed in the entrance and waited for Cynthia Griffin to notice. When she did, the woman's welcoming smile twitched, but to her credit, the smile stayed as if also permanently hand-painted.

"I thought you and Amanda could chat down here. Much more comfortable than up in her room."

Maggie didn't budge. She was already relinquishing home-field advantage to Amanda. She hated to give her anything more.

"She hardly ever comes down from that room these days," Mrs. Griffin said. She managed to keep the smile but there was a sadness that slipped into her tone. "All this has been so hard on her. She's just had a lot to deal with since Griff and I got married."

That's when Maggie realized Amanda might feel less comfortable in the family's formal living room than she did.

"Are any of those raspberry?" Maggie asked, pretending to be drawn in by the pastries and saving Mrs. Griffin from resorting to what Maggie dreaded might be her next step—begging.

"Oh yes. The ones with powdered sugar on top." The woman brightened and fluttered her spandex-clad arms like excited wings. Pouring coffee before Maggie could refuse. "Cream or sugar?"

"No, thank you. Black's fine," Maggie answered, rather than explain that she didn't drink coffee no matter what she put in it.

"Amanda loves this gourmet grind. Of course, she does. It's expensive." Mrs. Griffin laughed, a short burst of air that sounded like "hah."

Maggie felt sorry for her, a woman surrounded by beautiful expensive things, all of them by authentic designers, genuine gold-trims, the best-quality fabrics and woods, rare collector accessories of porcelain and ceramic—nothing artificial except her personality.

Maggie strolled the room while Mrs. Griffin crimped linen napkins and teased pastries onto the plates without disturbing powdered sugar or icing. Maggie scanned the display on the fireplace mantel, almost a dozen framed photos of different sizes and shapes. Amanda as a baby. Mrs. Griffin with her extended family, all dressed up and smiling. A wedding photo of Cynthia and Mike Griffin. More of Amanda in various stages of childhood. And then one photo caught Maggie's eye.

Three soldiers in military fatigues stood in front of a tank with a stark background that looked like miles and miles of sand. The one in the middle was a young Mike Griffin, his arms around the other two and smiling for the camera.

She almost glanced away, then realized the man on Griffin's left was also familiar. She took a closer look but there was no mistake. The man was Frank Skylar.

FIFTY-TWO

Wesley Stotter couldn't believe his eyes. He had already snapped more than fifty photos and was worried he'd run out of disc space on his digital camera.

He had brought along a pry bar but was surprised to find the back door unlocked. A keypad at the door implied security access. He suspected someone must be on the complex grounds and had stepped out for a minute; however, Stotter hadn't seen any movement. If he ran into a worker he'd pretend to be lost. What was that old saying, "It's easier to ask forgiveness than permission"?

The outside of the building had been so plain. Inside, Stotter was surprised to find whitewashed walls and an impressive labyrinth of stainless-steel counters topped with strange equipment and utensils that looked like a surgical suite. The counters were intersected with cylindrical tanks, some small, some large. Several stretched from floor to ceiling. They were filled with liquid and each had objects floating inside. All of them emitted an eerie blue glow—probably a fluorescent light somewhere inside each tank.

A built-in wall cabinet with a padlocked glass front displayed an array of other equipment that Stotter had never seen before. At first glance the stuff reminded him of something out of a *Star Wars* movie. Or—and this was what excited Stotter—perhaps weapons taken from a downed and disabled alien spacecraft. One appeared to be a scoped rifle but made of a strange metal and with an odd attachment on the barrel. At the stock, an electrical cord—only thicker—connected the rifle to what looked like a canvas backpack.

Hanging beside the rifle were several different pairs of goggles. Stotter squatted to study them. One pair had bulbous dark-green lenses with pinpoint red dots in each. Night-vision goggles, he suspected, and he wondered if these were what he had seen on the creature running in the forest. Was it only a man, after all?

Before he moved on to the next room he wanted to get closer shots of the tanks. He adjusted his camera to twilight mode so he could capture the images despite the fluorescent blue glow. He hadn't noticed until his fingers stumbled over the settings that his hands were shaking. His shirt had become glued to his back and his beard was damp with sweat as well.

He thought he heard a door open and he stopped.

Car stalled. Lost my way. He tried to prepare his story while he drew closer to the tanks. *Just fascinated by everything you have here*—that's what he would tell them. But he needed to stow the camera in his backpack or certainly they'd take it away from him.

He glanced around and didn't see anyone. Maybe it was his imagination again. An electrical motor began to hum and a fan above him came on. Stotter let out a breath and wiped his forehead. Of course, it was just the equipment turning on and off. But still he needed to be quick. He shouldn't press his luck.

In the first tank huge plant leaves floated, layers and layers of them. Gorgeous, unusual large leaves with blood-red veins running throughout. The liquid in the tank kept them perfectly preserved. He snapped a few photos and moved on to the next.

He stared for a few minutes at the next tank. Five very different objects, different sizes, shapes, and consistencies. They looked organic but almost translucent, the blue glow shining through in areas and highlighting what looked like a network of veins and blood vessels. Again he squatted to study them from below and that's when he recognized the object right in front of him. The shock made him jerk backward. His knees gave out and sent him sprawling. He dropped his camera and it skidded just out of reach.

Another motor turned on somewhere in the building, and yet Stotter didn't take his eyes off the object.

He hadn't been able to identify it at first. But even from this angle—his butt on the cold tile floor—Stotter could tell that what he was looking at was an eyeball.

He crawled to his knees, still not taking his eyes off the

tank and examining the other floating objects. Now he could make an educated guess as to what they were. He needed to focus as he tried to remember everything that was missing whenever a rancher found a mutilated cow. Because Stotter was pretty sure he had just found some of those missing pieces.

He continued staring as he reached out and searched for his camera. It had fallen close by. Still on his knees, he swiped his hand across the floor. That's when a heavy boot came down on his knuckles and Stotter heard the cracking of his own fingers.

His yelp of pain was cut short by a second boot that caught him under the chin and snapped his head back.

FIFTY-THREE

"Sheriff Skylar didn't mention that he served with your husband," Maggie said, noticing a second photo of the same three men, only in this one they wore hunting gear, including camouflage clothing. They stood next to a deer that had been strung up from a tree. Skylar and the other man held rifles. Mike Griffin stood in the middle again, holding one of the biggest hunting knives Maggie had ever seen.

"Oh yes." Mrs. Griffin came up beside Maggie and her index finger brushed the frame of the first photo. Her finger traveled down the length of the third man, a stranger Maggie didn't recognize. The gesture of affection seemed odd, but Maggie saw true emotion for the first time in Cynthia Griffin's face.

She glanced up at Maggie but didn't appear embarrassed or apologetic.

"Mike, Frank, and my first husband, Evan, served in Desert Storm," she explained. "This was taken right before

270

they came back. Unfortunately Evan didn't come home with them."

"I'm sorry to hear that."

"Evan and Griff were engineers. The National Guard was supposed to be just for playing weekend soldier. That's what Evan told me when he joined."

"Mom?"

Cynthia Griffin jumped and that was the last uncontrolled emotion Maggie would witness for the day.

"Oh, Mandy. Agent O'Dell wants to talk with you again."

"If this is about Courtney and Nikki, I don't know anything."

"No, I'm not here to ask you about them."

The girl couldn't disguise her relief though she tried to, pushing at her hair that, although washed and combed today, still fell conveniently into her eyes. Her skin looked healthier and her eyes weren't bloodshot, pupils not dilated.

Maggie waited for Mrs. Griffin to instruct her daughter where to sit and reminded her about the coffee being her favorite as she placed a cup on the matching saucer in front of Amanda.

"You haven't eaten anything all day." Mrs. Griffin fussed as she slid one of the beautiful pastries closer to her daughter.

"I don't want to talk about Johnny, either," Amanda said, but this time to her mother.

"Tell you what," Maggie said, coming around the glass

coffee table to sit across from Amanda, "I promise none of my questions will be about Johnny or Courtney or Nikki. I won't even ask about Thursday night."

Amanda peered out from under the strand of hair and this time she tucked it behind her ear.

"Okay," she agreed. "What do you want to know?"

"Tell me about Taylor Cole," Maggie said and watched Amanda's mouth drop open. "She was a friend of yours, right?"

Maggie didn't take her eyes off Amanda but she could see Mrs. Griffin half sit, half lean on the arm of a Queen Anne chair behind her.

"Yeah, I guess so." The girl pretended to shake off her surprise.

"You were with her when she jumped off the bridge?"

"I wasn't the only one."

"She didn't jump," Mrs. Griffin was quick to add. "It was an accident."

"I know about the salvia," Maggie said, letting that sink in along with Mrs. Griffin who now sank into a chair.

"I bet Dawson squealed, right?" Amanda said with a disgusted smirk.

"Taylor was your best friend until she graduated last spring." Maggie was careful not to say what she really believed, that Amanda felt like Taylor was leaving her behind, just like Johnny would do next year when he left to play football for a college possibly as far off as Florida or California.

Amanda shoved her plate away and Maggie knew her window of opportunity had just closed.

"Taylor didn't slip and fall off the bridge, did she? You were all flying high on salvia and someone dared her to jump."

"This is quite enough," Mrs. Griffin said, standing again though a bit wobbly. She scrambled in front of her daughter as if somehow protecting her. "Amanda, you do not have to talk about this. Agent O'Dell, you must leave."

Maggie didn't argue. But as she got up she noticed Amanda's forearm. The red marks had started to fade into a bluish-purple bruise.

"I'm not sure if your daughter knows who attacked them the other night," Maggie told Mrs. Griffin while she kept her eyes on Amanda. "I do know she's not telling you everything she does know. After I leave, you might want to ask her why she bit herself and pretended it was someone else."

Amanda's startled look confirmed Maggie's guess.

Back on the road, Maggie realized it was all beginning to make sense. Amanda was the one who orchestrated the drug parties. It was her way of keeping control over the friends she invited into her group. But when they threatened to leave she found a way to get back at them.

Maggie couldn't be sure that Amanda talked Johnny into committing suicide but the texts that she had read explained the pattern of their relationship. Had Amanda convinced him his future was over? That he would be stuck forever in the Nebraska Sandhills with her? Amanda probably didn't think the idea would drive Johnny to kill himself. Or did she?

When Dawson asked about Amanda after Maggie told him Johnny was dead, Maggie assumed he was concerned about the girl—maybe because he had a little bit of a crush on her. But now Maggie realized Dawson was scared when he asked, not concerned. He had wanted to know whether or not he still had to worry about Amanda's wrath. As for Courtney and Nikki? Maggie hadn't quite figured that out yet.

Nor had she figured out who had attacked the teenagers in the forest on Thursday night. Perhaps it wasn't related. But she wondered why Sheriff Frank Skylar chose to leave out the fact that Mike Griffin was a longtime friend when he conducted his interview of the man's stepdaughter. And did he manipulate the case of Taylor Cole to further protect Amanda?

Frank Skylar was also ex-military. If a laser stun gun like Donny or Platt described was used on these kids, it would have been obtained by someone who had military ties. Maybe it was a long shot to think Skylar had something to do with the attacks. But it did make Maggie wonder, what else was Sheriff Skylar not telling her?

FIFTY-FOUR

―――――

CHICAGO

O'HARE INTERNATIONAL AIRPORT

Platt and Bix didn't talk the entire trip from the north side of Chicago to O'Hare. They were stunned, exhausted, overwhelmed. Now, tucked away in the midst of a crowd of travelers, they finally felt safe.

Bix listened to his messages. Made a few calls. Platt bought a large coffee. He thought about getting something to eat but the smell of raw beef lingered in his nostrils.

Bix closed his phone and released a long breath, as if he had been holding it all day.

"There's a reason no one could identify this strain of salmonella," he said, shaking his head and rubbing his temples. "It changes."

"You said it might be a mutated strain," Platt said.

"No, I mean it changes once it's inside the human body.

275

Fifteen of the Norfolk victims that were released as okay two days ago are back in the hospital."

"Maybe it takes longer to leave the body in some victims."

"But they're telling me that six days later the bacteria itself looks different than it did on day four."

"Different, how?"

"Stronger. More resilient. It's like it's mutated to better survive and invade its new environment. It's clinging on to the wall of the intestines."

"It's not unusual to need some antibiotics with salmonella infection, especially if it hangs on or spreads."

"That's what they thought. So far, not much of a response."

"Antibiotic resistant?"

"Big-time."

"We'll need to come up with a cocktail of antibiotics."

"What if it's something they developed?" Bix asked in almost a whisper. "Tell me why that guy, Tegan, was so excited to see someone from USAMRIID. And what projects from the 1970s was he talking about?"

Philip Tegan had ended up giving them a short tour after realizing the two men he had allowed inside his facility might actually not be aware of all the classified work done in the laboratories despite their impressive credentials. He told them about the different hybrid crops they had been able to genetically engineer and he showed them—in excruciating detail—how they were able to do that. He informed them that 77 percent of soybeans are genetically engineered as is 85 percent of corn in the United States. The biotech crops decrease the use of pesticide, require less water, and reduce carbon that normally is released into the atmosphere. All good things for our environment.

When a skeptical Bix asked if it's healthy, Tegan reassured him that, of course, it was and that these crops were fed only to animals—not used for human consumption.

China, he told them, had created a new corn that contained an enzyme that makes pigs better able to digest the nutrient phosphorus, which would decrease the amount in their excrement. Phosphorus, he went on to explain, was the major polluter of waterways. "Isn't that amazing?"

But when Bix asked what happened to people when they ate the pork that ate the special corn, Tegan just laughed. "We'll have to wait and see, huh?"

Platt knew about the technology. He also knew Tegan's tour didn't include any of the labs they had seen soldiers guarding or those where they had seen an armored truck leaving. They wouldn't see those. At least not on this visit.

"So what was USAMRIID doing back in the 1970s?" Bix asked when Platt hesitated too long.

"During the Cold War, when there was a race to create ultimate weapons—before Russia and the United States signed a treaty agreeing to stop—USAMRIID had a program to develop bioweapons."

"Like mustard gas?"

"Like mustard gas. And anthrax. Other viruses that we might be able to launch on an entire population."

"Jesus!" Bix sputtered. "And now they're going to fucking do it with food?"

They sat side by side, staring straight ahead, waiting for their flight back to D.C. to be called.

"When your friend calls," Platt said, continuing to use their code word for the whistle-blower, no longer because it was necessary but now because it had become habit, "tell him we need to meet him face-to-face."

"He won't do that."

"Tell him he has to or we're calling a press conference."

FIFTY-FIVE

NEBRASKA

Maggie changed into shorts, a sweatshirt, and running shoes despite the setting sun and the beginning chill. She wanted to clear her head, drain some of the tension building into a knot between her shoulder blades.

She left a note for Lucy on the kitchen table, then she and Jake headed out on the road. By now the German shepherd understood this was for fun and not a flight from danger.

She had called Donny but got switched almost immediately to his voice mail. She wanted to tell him about Amanda and what she knew about Sheriff Skylar holding back evidence in the Taylor Cole case.

Through Maggie's limited resources she had learned that Taylor Cole had graduated last spring from the same county high school as the other teenagers and was planning to attend the University of Nebraska at Kearney. Her parents and friends all said she was the happiest they had ever seen her, excited and looking forward to embarking on her new adventure. No one would have predicted that she would choose to end her life by jumping off the Highway 83 Bridge and falling a hundred and fifty feet to her death, plunging into the fast and wild Middle Loup River below.

Of course, it had to be an accident. Though no one had an explanation for that, either. There were no eyewitness accounts. And no further investigation, as far as Maggie could tell. Kids tripping out on drugs was still only a rumor. Unfortunately, rumors usually had a grain of truth to them. And today Amanda confirmed those rumors were true.

Maggie understood a sheriff wanting to protect the reputation of a dead victim, maybe trying to protect the victim's loved ones. What was it that Lucy had said, that it could be devastating for parents to find out things about their dead child? Skylar may have thought, why put Taylor Cole's parents through that? They were already grieving the loss of their daughter. But in doing so, Skylar had let all the other teenagers involved off the hook.

Maggie saw Jake pin back his ears. He started herding her to the edge of the dirt road before she heard the faint rumble of an engine over the hill behind them. This time she listened to the dog and moved left to the crumbling edge. If the driver didn't see her until he came zooming down the hill, she would still be far enough to the left side that she would be safe. She had even worn a white T-shirt to be more visible in the fading daylight. But none of this calmed Jake.

She heard the engine getting closer, slowing down as it reached the top of the hill. She glanced back. The headlights prevented her from seeing beyond the windshield. It was a pickup truck or SUV, something riding high. Perhaps the same young man who had almost run her over the other day. It had slowed to a crawl. Overly cautious. Without looking back again, she waved her hand for the vehicle to go on by. She didn't break her pace and ignored Jake nudging her. But then she heard the dog growl.

She felt a sharp pain in the middle of her back before she realized that she had been hit. She fell to her knees. A jolt of electricity surged all the way through her. She tried to reach around to grab what had stabbed into her back, only her hands wouldn't move.

Couldn't move.

Why couldn't she move her arms, her hands, her fingers?

They didn't even brace her for the fall and her cheek slammed into the crusty sand. Her muscles started to spasm. Her body jerked beyond her control. Sand and gravel bit into her skin. Then her muscles locked up. Her head began to spin. But that was the only motion. She still couldn't move. She was paralyzed.

She heard Jake whimper and opened her mouth to tell him to run. Get out. Go home. But what came out was a babble of gibberish in a weak, tinny voice that she didn't recognize.

The boots appeared before her eyes. She hadn't heard their approach. Could no longer hear anything except her own heartbeat, the thumps inside a wind tunnel. She tasted sand and realized her mouth was open. She couldn't close it. Couldn't even look up. The world was spinning, tilted sideways. All she could see were the boots standing in front of her, mud-caked boots that smelled like river sludge.

FIFTY-SIX

___

Julia Racine threw the newspaper down on the bed beside Rachel. It didn't make the thump she had hoped but it was enough to draw Rachel's attention from her iPad and the annoying chatter of CNN pundits. She was already in bed in her nightshirt, covers pulled up to her waist, but her work still surrounded her, notepads, pens, news journals spilling onto Julia's side of the bed.

"You never read my column," Rachel said, glancing at the page of the newspaper that Julia had carefully folded back.

Julia was tired. She'd missed her day off only to have it followed by a long shift that included two drug dealers offing each other, doing the District a favor but leaving a bloody mess in the parking lot of a boarded-up and otherwise abandoned gas station. Of course, no one in the neighborhood had seen a thing. Then on break she happened to take a look at someone's discarded *Washington*

Post. And despite what Rachel thought, Julia did read her column as well as every investigative piece she had written since they met. Maybe she didn't always tell her that she read her stuff.

"You said you wouldn't use anything I told you."

"I didn't."

"Dumpster diving for evidence?"

"Okay, that was too colorful to skip but come on, I didn't say what was found."

"A late-night meeting with the USDA?"

"Now wait a minute." And this time Rachel put her iPad aside and sat up ready to defend herself. "I do have sources other than you, Julia."

"What sources do you know at the USDA who would have known about that late-night meeting?"

"Mommy." CariAnne appeared at the bedroom door, sleepy-eyed, pale, and dragging her favorite stuffed animal, a koala bear with one button eye missing.

"Just a minute, sweetie," Rachel told her, putting her hand out, palm up in total not-while-mommy's-talking mode. Until she saw the little girl's face. "What's wrong, sweetie?"

"I don't feel so good. I got the runnies."

Rachel was already out of bed.

"And I pooped red."

FIFTY-SEVEN

NEBRASKA

Maggie didn't know how she had gotten into the back of the SUV.

She did remember that there had been two more jolts of pain, each one more excruciating than the first. She had felt her eyes roll back in her head. Maybe she had passed out. She couldn't focus. Vision was blurry. So much pain had rocketed through her body. She remembered seeing her arms jump with each jolt but she had no control. Saw them flail and flap like a rag doll. Her back muscles had spasmed, tightened stiff, and locked in position until the next jolt of electricity jammed its way through.

Now as she lay in the back of the vehicle, her chest ached. It hurt to breathe. Her pulse raced—*too fast, way too fast.* Her throat was raw and dry—so dry—she couldn't swallow. And yet, her mouth hung open. She felt drool sliding down her chin.

She stared at the ceiling of the vehicle. She saw her knees bunched up beside her. At least she thought they were her knees. She couldn't feel them. Her hands were in front of her, bound at the wrists by a zip tie. She had no idea if her feet were bound together. She couldn't see or feel them, either.

A voice droned on and on. It reverberated, hollow and muffled from somewhere above her head. Or was it inside her head? She didn't recognize it. The radio?

" . . . should have headed back to Denver."

No, it was him. He was talking about her. Talking to her. From the front seat, right above her head. But he sounded like he was miles away at the other end of a tunnel. She could only decipher bits and pieces of what he was saying.

The vehicle started turning and she slid. Something thumped against the wall beside her. A clank of metal rang in her ears. The tires switched from pavement to dirt, hard and rutted. Her body bounced and her head banged. A wave of nausea came over her and she started to panic. If she vomited she wouldn't be able to roll over. She'd choke. She felt dizzy and looked for something to focus on. Like Dawson, she needed something to keep her eyes on, to concentrate on.

Outside the window she saw deep, dark-blue sky and a few blurred glitters. Twilight. How could it already be so dark?

Another turn. Another clank.

Maggie twisted her head so she could continue to see the

sky. In doing so she also got a glimpse of what clanked beside her.

Oh, God, it was a shovel.

The nausea became strong. Her panic continued to rise up.

Star light, star bright. First star I see tonight.

She found a twinkling star in the deep sea of twilight and she held on.

FIFTY-EIGHT

Platt didn't have time to drive home from the airport. Instead he and Bix had dinner in the District. Old Ebbitt Grill was one of Maggie's favorites. The men needed somewhere convenient and close to the monuments. He thought of the restaurant immediately and now he was glad.

It felt good to be surrounded by the warm glow of the antique gaslights and the thought of Maggie laughing from across the table. She and Gwen Patterson came here all the time, but she had brought him once. Corner booth. It had been steamy outside. Cool inside. Beers and burgers and a lively discussion about Spencer Tracy and Katharine Hepburn movies.

Tonight the high-backed booths would allow Platt and Bix some privacy. And because they weren't politicos who frequented the place, they wouldn't be recognized or noticed. Sure enough—no one even turned to look at them.

Platt ordered a Sam Adams. Bix frowned at him and ordered coffee.

"We aren't meeting him for two hours," Platt said. "I think I can have a beer."

Bix continued to scowl.

"You should have beer, too."

"I don't drink."

"You might start after today."

"We need to eat. I haven't eaten all day." Bix pulled open the menu.

"No red meat. Okay? It might be a long time before I have another cheeseburger."

Platt's cell phone interrupted just as they finished placing their orders with the waiter. He went to hit Ignore but then he saw it was his parents' number. He hadn't checked in with them since yesterday. It'd be his father. He knew that his mother always nagged—"Call your son."

"Hi, Dad." He glanced at his watch. Not quite time yet for their late-night shows.

"Ben, so are you back home or still in Chicago?"

No one but Bix knew he had gone to Chicago. He hadn't even told anyone at USAMRIID.

"How'd you know I was in Chicago, Dad?"

Bix looked up across the table, setting down his coffee so hard he splashed some on his hand and didn't bother to wipe at it.

"A friend of yours stopped by here."

Platt's stomach lurched.

"What friend?"

"Military guy. Said you asked him to check up on us."

"Did he give you a name?"

"Jack ... oh, what was his last name. Your mother would remember. Scared us at first because he was in uniform. We were worried something might have happened to you. But he said you were okay. He was just checking on us while you were in Chicago. So how was Chicago?"

It was a warning. If they wanted to hurt his parents they could have already done it. That was exactly what they were telling him, letting him know that they could hurt them at any given moment. It would be worthless to tell his parents to pack up and leave. Go to a hotel, a resort. No place would be safe. His heart raced while his mind played out scenario after scenario, none of them good. He would make a phone call to USAMRIID and within a couple of hours, he would have a real friend outside his parents' home, watching for him.

"Chicago was fine," he finally answered.

"Colder than here, I bet."

"Wetter. It rained the whole time." He tried to keep his tone even so it wouldn't betray him.

"Well, I'm glad you're back, safe and sound. And listen, your mom and me are fine. You really don't need to send anyone to check on us. We'll be just fine."

"I know, Dad."

"We love you, son."

"Love you, too." He ended the call and placed his cell phone on the table.

It was Bix who broke the silence.

"Holy son of a bitch. What the hell did we step in?"

FIFTY-NINE

NEBRASKA

Maggie's view of the sky and her star got blocked out by canopy after canopy of trees. They were in the forest, thumping along roads that weren't well traveled. Branches scraped the roof of the vehicle and pine needles brushed the windows.

He was going to bury her out here, someplace deep in the woods where hikers and hunters never went. He couldn't have just killed her on the road where she was running. Someone might have come along. Besides he'd have gotten blood all over the back of his SUV. So he used a Taser. Her body still remembered the pain.

Had to be a Taser.

The darts had clawed into her back through her shirt. All he had to do was simply lean out his window and fire. She had been an easy target. Once the darts hit and grabbed onto her back, the electrical charge would race through the wires attached to the gun. He controlled how long the charge would last. A few seconds incapacitated a victim. She went down immediately. No fight. No struggle. The additional charges, at that point, were strictly for pain.

Her spinning mind had started to unravel what had happened. She still couldn't figure out who was in the driver's seat. Who wanted her incapacitated and in pain? Who wanted her dead?

Her muscles ached. But that was good. That meant the feeling was coming back into them. The temporary paralysis was wearing off. She didn't think he had tied her feet together. They felt loose but she couldn't quite feel them. No, he probably didn't tie them. He'd need her to walk. Even if it was a stumble, he'd want her on her feet so he could take her deeper into the forest. It'd be easier than carrying or dragging her. Yes, he'd make her walk to her own grave site.

Maggie tried to wiggle her fingers. They tingled. Tingling was good. She saw her hands, zip-tied together on her stomach, only when the brake lights flared up in the dark. At first, she was almost surprised to see they were still connected to her. In the red glow her body looked twisted and broken.

Her skull roared. Every time she lifted her head it felt like it would explode. But her vision wasn't quite as blurry and the nausea was less. Her heartbeat had slowed. It no longer felt like it would gallop out of her chest. Even the ringing in her ears had subsided.

Better. She was doing better. But then the SUV came to a stop.

The engine shut down. Parking lights stayed on. She heard the driver's door open. No dinging. He took the keys with him. Slammed the door shut. The dome light hadn't come on. He must have shut it off earlier.

Darkness surrounded the vehicle. In the glow of the parking lights she could see trees and thick brush all around them. Even the road was not really a road. The vehicle had cut the first path through the tall grass, squeezing between tree trunks. Maggie wondered how he'd back out of here. An odd thing to care about for someone who knew she was not going to be leaving with him.

He'd expect her to still be dazed and incapacitated. He wouldn't be disappointed.

The tailgate clicked and her body jerked. She told herself that was another good sign but her heart started pounding again.

The hinges screeched and the tailgate went up. In the glow of the parking lights she saw Mike Griffin with his hunting knife.

SIXTY

Platt had always thought the Washington monuments were at their most awesome at night. The bright spotlights cast halos in the dark and the guided tours drew whispered reverence from the tourists—that didn't happen in the daylight.

The whistle-blower had agreed to meet them at the FDR Memorial. In the movies wasn't it always the Lincoln Memorial? But now Platt saw the wisdom. FDR's was all ground level, no steps to get trapped on. There were separate sections, actually what they called "rooms," but even that was beneficial. The person could wander through each, bypassing Bix and Platt at will if he didn't feel comfortable.

Bix traded his suit jacket and Platt his uniform jacket for Smithsonian sweatshirts. Bix carried their folded jackets in a paper bag with the Smithsonian logo, making them look like tourists.

"So how long do we give him to find us?" Platt asked.

"He's only ten minutes late." Bix checked his watch. "Twelve minutes."

Platt still didn't like this idea but they had no choice. He wouldn't be surprised if the whistle-blower ended up being someone from the media: a reporter wanting to confirm his tips. Maybe Bix didn't mind being sent on wild-goose chases but Platt was tired of it. Especially when the chase might involve his parents.

They were staring at one of the walls, neither of them reading the engravings, when a woman came up beside Bix. As long as tourists kept coming and going, their guy would probably stay away. Platt elbowed Bix and nodded for them to move on just as the woman said, "Good evening, gentlemen."

Both men did a double take. What the hell was Irene Baldwin doing here? They were so busted. Had she followed them?

Bix glanced around and Platt knew he was looking to see if they had just scared away the whistle-blower.

"Hello, Ms. Baldwin," Platt finally said when it became obvious that Bix couldn't find his voice.

"How's the weather in Chicago?"

That was the line. How did she know the line the anonymous caller said he would use?

Then Platt took a good look at her. She, too, was wearing

a Smithsonian sweatshirt, jeans, her usual swept-up hair now flowing over her shoulders. Even the eyeglasses were new. Had it not been for her distinctive voice he wasn't sure he would have recognized her.

"You?" Bix asked. "What the hell's going on?"

SIXTY-ONE

NEBRASKA

"This is where you get out, O'Dell."

Griffin grabbed Maggie's ankles and started to pull.

She couldn't stop him. Her feet wouldn't listen to her head telling them to kick. She could barely feel his fingers grabbing her around the ankles. With her wrists tied she couldn't stop him and she couldn't break the two-foot fall from the tailgate to the ground.

She landed hard on her right shoulder, hard enough that she thought she must have dislocated it. A fresh wave of pain spiked through her upper body. Better that she came down on her shoulder than her head. The pain didn't subside and she immediately thought, maybe not better. A tingling sensation spread all the way down to her toes.

He obviously didn't care how banged up she got now. He'd simply bury any mess he made. He dragged her all the way to the edge of the ridge. She could see only far enough in the dark to know it was a steep drop-off. She remembered climbing down to get to the crime scene. One wrong step and you'd fall until you hit a tree. He left her within a foot of tumbling over. It didn't matter. There would be no crime-scene techs, no coroner, not even the county attorney to figure out all the marks on her body, because her body would never be found.

Now he didn't look pleased that she couldn't stand up. He'd done too good of a job with the Taser. She saw him looking around, devising a new strategy, glancing at his clothing. He went back to the SUV, keeping an eye on her as he looked into the back of the vehicle. He was big enough, strong enough to carry her. But that was obviously not what he wanted to do. He hadn't dressed for the occasion. Maybe he'd been in a hurry. He didn't want to risk getting anything from her on his clothing.

Had he heard about her visit with Amanda? Is that what pushed him to do this?

"Why?" she managed to ask. Her mouth was dry. She could taste metal. She wasn't sure if he could even hear her. But it stopped him.

"I just wanted to scare those kids," he said, looking at her as he dug inside a tool kit he'd found in the back of the SUV. "They kept snooping around the field house. I told Amanda to stay the fuck away."

So it had been Mike Griffin that night with a laser stun gun.

"I've got a sweet deal here. I'm not about to lose it."

"They'll look for me," she said and realized immediately how lame it sounded.

"Twenty thousand acres of valleys and hills and all covered with trees and thick brush. This time of year, pine needles dropping, leaves dropping over everything. In less than a month there'll be snow. They might look"—he stopped, squinted because she was no longer in the halo of the parking lights, and tried to meet her eyes—"but they won't find you."

In that instant, Maggie realized this wasn't a man to reason with. She'd met killers face-to-face before. She recognized that empty, hollowed-out stare. When they looked at you like you were an object to be removed—an object and not a person—it was already too late.

Griffin put one knee up onto the tailgate and half climbed into the back of the SUV, pulling out shovel, tarp, and rope for his readjusted plan. Easier to bury tarp and ropes than his clothes. His back was slightly turned to her. He didn't need to worry about her running away when she had just proven she couldn't even protect her shoulder from hitting the ground.

But that thump must have jolted more than just her collarbone. She could feel her feet. She could feel her hands and her fingers. And they actually worked when she wanted them to flex and move.

Griffin clanked around in the back of his SUV. He didn't have to worry about sounds out here, either. Hank and the rest of the forest rangers were miles away. Maggie used his noise to cover her scuffs and intakes of breaths. She bit her lower lip to stop any groans.

Her mind raced. She'd never be able to take him down. Not with her wrists tied. Not with her muscles weak and her skull spinning. The keys were in his pocket but she'd never be able to get them and make it into the SUV without him being on top of her. She couldn't even swing the shovel at him.

She saw him crawl deeper inside the back of the SUV. Then she did the only thing she could. She took a deep breath and rolled over the edge of the ridge.

SIXTY-TWO

WASHINGTON, D.C.

Platt, Bix, and Baldwin found a bench a few feet away from the monument, out of tour guides' path as they led their groups. And hopefully out of earshot.

"The meat-processing plant you visited is notorious for contaminated beef," Baldwin explained. "And yet the Department of Agriculture keeps giving them chance after chance to clean up their act."

"Aren't they supposed to close them down after so many offenses?"

"Oh, they have. For a day or two. They clean everything. Get it all spotless and sterile. But in case you didn't notice, processing beef is a messy business. I'm always surprised that there aren't more contaminations."

"And some of this plant's contaminated beef ended up in the National School Lunch Program."

"Three orders were purchased in late August by the

302

USDA. I thought it was ridiculous to continue to buy from this vendor with their track record, but I'm the new kid."

"Can you track those orders and see what schools received them?" Platt asked but he already knew it couldn't be that easy or they wouldn't be here.

"Once they get sent to state warehouses it's almost impossible to track where they go. I've discovered the NSLP is a complex maze of illogical proportions."

"So a recall?"

Baldwin bristled, her back straightening. She let out a sigh, more frustration than relief. "I realized the day after the Norfolk, Virginia, outbreak that I wouldn't be able to do anything from inside."

"Wait a minute," Bix said. "You knew about the outbreak the day after?"

"Yes. How do you suppose it came about that you finally were called in?"

Bix crossed his arms over his chest and Platt saw that his right foot had started tapping out his anger.

"Did you know immediately that it was an unusual strain of salmonella?" Platt asked.

"Yes."

"And still there weren't any notices sent to schools?" Now Platt was having a difficult time tamping down his anger.

"That's the part you don't understand." Another long intake of breath. She rubbed at the back of her neck. In the faint light from the monument Platt could see the lines at her eyes and mouth. She wasn't wearing any makeup. "They want to contain this one quietly. They want it to go away unnoted and chalk it up as just another contamination. When they came to me last week they said they had it under control."

"You didn't believe them," Bix said. "So you made sure I was on the case."

"I knew immediately when I heard about the elementary school in the District that it had to be related. And that there would be others."

"How did you know already that it was an unusual strain of salmonella?" Platt asked.

"Because they told me the exact strain they had created and put in."

SIXTY-THREE

NEBRASKA

The first ten feet were the worst. A sharp drop straight down sent Maggie falling into a black abyss. A ledge caught her, pine needles breaking the impact. Somehow she had managed to not cry out though she landed on her right shoulder again. If Griffin had heard the scuffle it would only be seconds, maybe a minute if she was lucky, before he realized where she had gone.

She forced her eyes to adjust to the darkness. Even the parking lights didn't add a glow of illumination. She knew the ridge continued down, she just didn't know how far. She pushed up to her knees and tested the small ledge she had landed on. Then she turned around, started scooting down on her butt, feetfirst, testing and feeling. It wasn't quite as steep.

She glanced up. Still no flashlight aimed down to find her. She allowed herself to slide, bracing her hands in front of her. She wouldn't be able to grab onto much but she could protect her face and head from slamming into a tree.

The sand gave way and she began to skid. She lost her balance. Her body twisted and she was sliding on her side.

Too fast, way too fast.

Branches lashed out, stabbing and scraping her skin. She needed to slow down, but she couldn't get a grip. Couldn't stop. Her bound wrists kept her from grabbing a rock or branch. Her hands became fists trying to protect and getting battered. Her body became a toboggan rolling over anything in its way, her hip bumping a tree trunk and sending her up against another. Branches snapped and cracked, stinging her arms, whipping at her face, catching her hair.

Then suddenly she landed a second time. On her back.

She stared up at the pine trees. In the complete darkness the patches of sky were bright with twinkling stars. She saw the top of the ridge above her. Dear God, it had to be at least sixty feet, more than six stories tall.

In the silence she heard an owl and the constant hum of cicadas. She lay perfectly still, knocked out of breath, certain that if she lifted her head she'd feel the dizziness at full force.

A branch snapped. Somewhere to the left of her there was a rustle of leaves. She forced herself to stay quiet, to not move. It wasn't possible. Griffin couldn't have made it to the bottom of the ridge before her.

Just an animal, she told herself. Then in the same breath she remembered it could be a coyote or cougar.

Calm down. Please heart, stop racing. Breathe. You need to breathe.

Her body ached. Her knuckles and elbows were scraped raw and bleeding. The zip tie had dug into her wrists and cut deep. The pain in her shoulder burned. But she had made it to the bottom. She'd gotten away.

That's when she saw the beam of a flashlight sweep over the ridge.

SIXTY-FOUR

"Their original intent was honorable," Baldwin tried to explain. "A war without soldiers. Isn't that the wave of the future?"

"What the hell are you talking about?" Bix hadn't recovered from his anger.

"Genetically engineered bioweapons," Platt said in almost a whisper. It was exactly what he and Bix had discussed at the airport.

"I understand you visited the facility next door." Baldwin paused but she wasn't waiting for their acknowledgment. It was as if she was deciding what and how much to reveal. "There are similar facilities across the country. Most of them independently contracted so the government can deny they exist. All of them hidden in plain sight. Some as small as a field house in one of our federal parks or a test field in the middle of a farmer's corn crop."

"So this contamination was intentional," Platt said.

"Yes."

"Son of a bitch." Bix palmed his forehead and shook his head.

"But it was not intended for schoolchildren. Someone made a mistake on one of the three orders. It was not supposed go to the NSLP."

"Where was it supposed to go?" Bix asked.

"I honestly don't know."

"Right."

"I came to this party late. They're not going to tell me those details. But I do know this much—it wasn't supposed to stay here in the United States."

"How did they think they'd get away with this?" Bix asked. "We have higher standards on our beef and poultry exports than on our imports. And our trading partners certainly wouldn't accept contaminated beef."

"Even in the best of systems it slips by, especially if it's a new strain no one is testing for. Why do you think they chose a processing plant that tests for bacterium so often? Plausible deniability."

Bix couldn't restrain his anger any longer. "You know the teenagers that recovered in Norfolk are becoming ill again? This bacterium is mutating, changing ... oh, but wait, that's exactly what it was engineered to do, right?"

Baldwin didn't answer. Bix didn't expect her to.

He continued: "Why send us to Chicago? Why not tell me all this that first day?"

"I was told it was being taken care of. Don't you understand? I was told to stand down by my superior. You remember who my boss's boss is."

She calmed herself down and glanced over her shoulder. The last of the tours had trouped through long ago.

"His boss is the president of the United States. It's not like I can just go knock on his door and say, 'Oh hey, by the way. That bioweapons program your secretary of agriculture and your secretary of defense developed, it almost killed over one hundred schoolkids.'"

"Might still kill them," Platt said. Bix's scientists were busy coming up with an antibiotic cocktail, hoping to combat the strain before it caused irreparable damage.

"What do you expect us to do?" Bix asked.

"I'm just a new undersecretary. But if the CDC and USAMRIID, along with the United States Army, take charge? Maybe it'll make a difference."

"Tell us what you want us to do," Platt said before Bix could argue.

SIXTY-FIVE

The darkness gave Maggie an advantage. Down here the moonlight broke through in rare streaks which Maggie tried to avoid. Her eyes had adjusted but some parts of the forest floor remained too dark to see. She still had to depend on her other senses, feeling her way as much as seeing.

When had it gotten so cold? It seeped beneath her shirt. And why had she worn shorts? Her knees were scraped raw, her legs scratched and bleeding. She heard her teeth chattering. She needed to keep moving.

The ache had not left her chest, but the night sounds worked to her advantage as well. The constant chirp of cicadas covered her raspy breathing and the crackling of dried leaves underfoot. She felt like someone was watching her. Stalking her. It couldn't be Griffin. She could still see the jumps of the flashlight beam shooting over the ridge. He hadn't come down, instead trying to find her from above.

At first he called her name. Made promises that quickly turned to taunts. Then he cursed her. But he didn't venture down the steep slope. She wasn't naïve enough to think that she had an edge on him. He knew this forest. He would know a shortcut, guess her direction.

She had recognized the goggles in the back of the SUV—infrared night vision. Could he see her? Was it that easy to track her movement? Maybe he was simply waiting for the right time to pounce. Perhaps he was letting her run out of energy. She'd put up less of a fight. She expected him at every turn. Thought she saw a shadow standing behind trees. Swore she could hear his footsteps catching up with her.

She wanted to hide, find someplace she could curl into a tight ball. Bury herself under branches and leaves. Keep herself warm with pine needles. Wait until morning. Her muscles screamed at her to do just that. The pain in her shoulder had taken on a life of its own. She tried to block it out.

Breathe. Keep moving. Listen. It became her mantra.

When she came out into a clearing she skidded to a stop. She saw a building, but no movement. No lights. She moved back into the forest, hid behind a tree, and stared at the corrugated metal. It was like a mirage. She wondered if she might be seeing things.

Then she remembered—there was a nursery out here. And a field house. Lucy had told her about it. She couldn't remember what it was. The Taser had blocked off portions of her memory.

She tried to concentrate. Griffin had said something about the field house. That he wanted to keep the teenagers away from it. Why? She couldn't remember. It didn't matter. He had a connection to this place. He had to know she would stumble across it. That she'd be tempted to consider it as a shelter. In fact, he probably counted on it.

And yet, she had to believe there would be something inside she could use to cut her wrists free. *And warmth*. If only for a few minutes.

SIXTY-SIX

Julia hated hospitals. She told Rachel she'd wait outside the exam room but the crowded ER made her feel even more anxious. Her mother had died in a place like this. Almost twenty years had passed and they still looked the same. It was as if she were seeing it through the eyes of a ten-year-old girl, instead of those of a homicide detective.

Across from her a woman cradled her bleeding arm. Knife wound. Under the thin stained gauze Julia recognized a tear in the flesh. Probably a kitchen knife, serrated blade. All she needed was a glance at the red-faced man accompanying the woman to guess it had been a domestic case, an endgame compromise—I'll forgive you but you have to take me to the emergency room to get patched up. No incident report would be filed. The exhausted intern would ask the volley of questions but end up writing in whatever "accident" the woman invented.

Julia was moving on to the next victim when Rachel stepped out of the exam room. Her eyes were wild and frantic and searching for Julia.

It took Julia a second or two before she could stand. *Oh God, this can't be good.*

She couldn't remember the last time her knees actually wobbled. Is this what being in a relationship was all about—anxiety, stress, fear? Why did she think she was missing out on something? She had been fine on her own. *Just fine.*

No, that's not, true. *You were lonely,* she told herself.

She weaved her way through the line waiting for the desk clerk. She steeled herself, the way she did when entering a crime scene. This was different. So different.

The relief on Rachel's face when she finally saw her made Julia's stomach fall to her feet. She was looking to her partner for strength. That expectation, that obligation fell like a weight on Julia's shoulders. She couldn't do this. Didn't have it in her.

Rachel reached for her hands.

"They're running an IV. CariAnne's really dehydrated." Rachel's lower lip trembled. There was something more. Julia could see it in her eyes. "They said other kids from the school are ill, too. They won't tell me what all is going on." She shot a look over her shoulder, not wanting CariAnne to hear her. "It's bad. I think it's really bad," she whispered.

Her grip on Julia's hands was so tight it hurt.

"I can't lose her," Rachel said.

"You're not going to lose her."

In the past Julia had always left herself escape hatches. She constructed them almost as soon as she entered a relationship. It was—she truly believed—a smart survival tactic. She never allowed herself to feel so much that she couldn't resurface. She was Houdini, looking out for number one because if she didn't, who would?

"Go back in with CariAnne," she told Rachel.

"I'm so scared. Come with me."

Julia cringed. So this was what it felt like to have your heart break.

"I'll be right here," she told Rachel. "There's something I have to do."

She was surprised how convincing she sounded. Rachel nodded, wiped her face, took one more squeeze of Julia's hands, and went back to her daughter.

Julia leaned against the wall. She sucked in gulps of disinfected air. When she pulled out her cell phone, her fingers shook so much she could barely hit the correct numbers.

The phone rang forever and she was torn between anger and frustration. He wouldn't recognize her number. *Please don't send me to voice message.* She wouldn't know what to say and she wouldn't have the nerve to call again.

Finally an answer.

"This is Benjamin Platt."

"I need a favor," she said, forgetting to even tell him who was calling.

SIXTY-SEVEN

NEBRASKA

When Maggie finally cut the zip tie it didn't immediately fall
from her wrists. Blood had caked and dried around it, and
she had to dig the plastic strip out of the deep groove it had
cut into her flesh. She found alcohol under one of the stainless-steel counters. Opened the bottle, held her breath, and
poured it onto her first wrist. She closed her eyes tight and
almost bit through her lower lip trying to silence her scream.

Don't pass out. You cannot pass out.

The second wrist was easier. Everything would be easier
now that her hands were free.

She hadn't needed any light once inside the field house.
Her eyes had quickly adjusted to the glow from several
tanks distributed throughout. Without much effort she had
discovered a pair of pruning shears. It had taken several
attempts at handling the shears before she cut the plastic
tie.

Now she stashed the shears in the pocket of her shorts and hunted for a better weapon.

One section of the building looked like a high-tech laboratory. Another section looked like a small processing center. Opening the thick glass doors Maggie immediately felt the difference. A gust of warm, dry air hit her in the face. It smelled of dirt and plants.

A blue fluorescent track lit up paths in the floor similar to those on commercial airplanes. It was enough to maneuver through the maze. And enough to see the clusters of plants hanging to dry from the ceiling.

Maggie didn't venture far into the room. There would be nothing here to help her. But as she turned to leave she recognized a bundle of leaves hanging in the rows of drying plants. Even in the fluorescent light she was pretty sure the leaves were similar to the ones in the plastic bag Lucy had found at the crime scene hidden underneath one of the boys. The size of the leaf, the shape—and what she could make out of the color—looked like *Salvia divinorum*.

Back in the main section of the building Maggie quickly made her way around the counters, opening drawers while watching both doors on the opposite side of the room. Huge fans turned on and off overhead obscuring her ability to hear. Someone could already be inside and she wouldn't know until he came up behind her. She focused on her other senses. She could smell something wet and musty and saw that her running shoes were caked with a wet sandy mud.

Earlier inside the SUV, she remembered that same odor. Had it come from Mike Griffin's boots?

Didn't Dawson say he could smell river mud? Now she understood where it came from.

Maggie tried to get a sense of where in the forest she was. What did Griffin tell her? He just wanted to scare the kids. Didn't want them snooping around the field house. This had to be where they had gotten the salvia. If he wanted to frighten them away, that meant the field house was close to the crime scene.

She couldn't spend any more time inside. She had already exceeded what she told herself was past high risk. She started to zigzag her way to the back door and that's when she found the tall cabinet with glass doors, holding a contraption that looked like a rifle.

She went to get a closer look, stepping around one and then another stainless-steel counter. She didn't see the foot, didn't see the man hunched on the floor until she was on top of him. She jumped back, ready to run. But the man didn't move.

In the blue glow she could see his face—eyes wide open, blood trickling from his mouth. Without checking she knew Wesley Stotter was dead.

SIXTY-EIGHT

She had to keep moving.

Don't stop. Don't look back.

She could do this. That's what Maggie told herself as she stumbled under the weight of the backpack with the rifle slung over her shoulder. Up ahead she saw the yellow crime-scene tape flapping from several trees. Just the sight pumped another surge of adrenaline. She could do this. She couldn't think about Stotter right now. She had to focus on the task at hand.

She had fired an assortment of weapons. How much different could this be from an AK-47? Except that it was very different with cords and packs and an energy source instead of bullets. But she wouldn't have time to study it. Lugging it was challenge enough. She had also helped herself to a pair of dirty white coveralls she found hanging by the door. She had rolled up the cuffs and the sleeves, pulling it over her shorts and sweatshirt. The warmth helped her ignore the extra bulk.

As soon as she left the field house she thought she heard

him. Leaves crackled, a branch snapped. Griffin wouldn't even need night-vision goggles to track her. But why let her leave with the rifle?

Because he doesn't think you'll be able to fire it.

She pushed the thought out of her mind.

For a rare moment the cicadas were quiet but Maggie couldn't hear Griffin. Again, he was giving her a head start.

Cocky son of a bitch.

She thought she heard a car door slam but she could no longer see the field house or the clearing. He knew she wouldn't get far. He'd stop and get what he needed.

Within minutes she made it past the yellow tape. She was back at the crime scene. Familiar territory. She could, at least, stay put, get set. But there were a few things she needed to do. She hoped she had enough time.

Without much effort she found what she was looking for. She tried to remember what Donny had told her, then she took a deep breath and got to work.

She saw Griffin without effort. He had put on a pair of the white coveralls, too. Which meant he was ready to do whatever it took. She imagined what the teenagers saw that night when he came for them. Dawson talked about a white wolf. Griffin had known the salvia would provide enough hallucinatory effects to enhance his disguise. This time he didn't have the bug-eyed goggles. He wouldn't need them. Maggie had counted on his confidence. That's why she chose the darkest shadows she could find, though she knew her white coveralls would be easy to spot.

"It's over," he told her, stopping about twenty feet away.

She raised the rifle and flipped the switch which sounded similar to racking a round of a shotgun.

She waited.

His steps were slow but not hesitant.

Her finger stayed on the trigger. Just a few more feet. She wanted to make sure he was in range for the full impact. She remembered Platt saying fifteen to twenty feet. She'd make him come as close as possible. She had checked all the connections, made sure the cord from the backpack to the rifle butt hadn't been disengaged. There were no other switches. She had checked.

Fifteen feet.

The darkness played to her disadvantage now. She couldn't see his face. Couldn't tell if he was afraid or smiling. She couldn't even make out what he was holding.

It was way too dark.

"Won't make a difference without the power pack," he said and held up an object.

Maggie felt as if she had been kicked in the gut. That was the one thing that was different about the rifle. It required an energy source in place of bullets. That's what the backpack was for. Was Griffin bluffing? Did the gun also need a power pack–like battery to hold its charge?

He stepped closer.

She ignored her sweaty palms and steeled herself. He had to be bluffing.

"Stop or I'll shoot."

He kept coming and Maggie pulled the trigger.

Nothing.

She tried again and the empty click made her heart stop. She heard him laugh as she threw down the rifle and clawed at the straps of the heavy backpack, trying to shrug it off as she turned to run.

He lunged at her. Didn't even see the wire she had strung chest-high between the two trees in front of her. He flew backward, knocked off his feet.

She was on him in seconds, flipping his body over. His muscles were stiff and contracted from the electrical shock. He didn't move when she slammed her knee into the small of his back. His arms jerked but he had no control over them as Maggie yanked them back and used zip ties she had found in the building.

He mumbled and jabbered, not unlike Dawson.

"Y-y-you b-i-i-i-i-tch."

He was much bigger than Dawson. The effects of the shock wouldn't last long. Maggie moved quickly to his feet, tying them together with the ropes they had used to secure the crime scene.

"Not get a-a-a-a-way."

She ignored him. Sweat drenched the inside of her coveralls. Her fingers were steady now, and she quickly grabbed another rope to connect the zip tie on his wrists to the rope on his feet. Then she pulled tight until he was bent in half.

"Damnit, y-y-you."

Hog-tied, he wasn't going anywhere. He could yell all he

wanted. She didn't hesitate and wrapped what was left of the rope around a tree.

"Nice job." A voice startled her from behind.

She spun around. Blinded by a flashlight, she still recognized the silhouette and the voice.

"No thanks to you," she told Sheriff Frank Skylar.

"It-it-it's about tim-m-m-me," Griffin stuttered.

Maggie shot a look back at Skylar. Only now did she see the sheriff had his weapon pointed at her.

"You really should have gone back to Denver," Skylar told her. "We would have handled this just fine. No one else would have had to be hurt."

"Sho-sho-shoot her."

Maggie stayed down on her haunches, unarmed. With the light blinding her, she couldn't even find a branch or rock.

"Now we're gonna have to make up some story about how that Stotter guy was stalking you. Shame the way things happen," Skylar was saying. "Both of you come up missing at the same time."

"He wasn't stalking me," Maggie said, wondering if it would make a difference if she tried to stall. Her muscles started screaming again, reminding her what they'd been through.

"Yeah, well, it's funny how rumors get started."

"Sho-sho-shoot her."

"Shut up," Skylar yelled. "I'm sick and tired of cleaning up after you. Why didn't you just stay in Chicago? You and your lamebrain scams."

He reached out and placed the gun barrel against her temple. The metal felt cold and solid.

She looked up, forcing him to look into her eyes, though she couldn't see his face. All she saw was a huge swatch of black fur hurling through the air just as the gun went off.

Maggie felt the heat scorch her skin. Pain ripped across the side of her skull. She fell hard against the ground. Couldn't hear anything except a high-pitched ring. The world swirled around her. From where she lay she could see Skylar's body twisting and turning. His mouth was open but she couldn't hear his screams, just the ringing inside her head. She saw Skylar cradling the bloody mess that used to be his arm.

She closed her eyes, expecting darkness, almost welcoming unconsciousness.

That's when she felt the warm wetness on her cheek.

She opened her eyes to find a huge black German shepherd licking her face.

MONDAY, OCTOBER 12

SIXTY-NINE

Julia Racine juggled a tray with two coffees, two chocolate doughnuts, one glazed cruller, and one container of chocolate milk while pinning a copy of *The Washington Post* under one arm and a stuffed koala bear under the other. A nurse helped her push open the door.

"Thanks," Julia said and bounded down the hall.

By now she was getting used to the smell of disinfectant and the ding of monitors inside dimly lit rooms. She kept herself from glancing into the rooms. She didn't want to see any other patients except CariAnne.

She found the girl and her mother mesmerized by yet another cable news show blaring the current events of the day. The anchor was discussing an impending press conference about the contaminated food in schools.

"Yah! Doughnuts!" both daughter and mother squealed, raising their arms.

"And you brought my bear."

CariAnne reached for the ragged stuffed animal but her left arm was still connected to a monitor. She stopped, readjusted, and tried again.

They were told all of the gizmos were only for precaution. So far the little girl was testing negative for all the salmonella strains they had been tracking. The antibiotic cocktail that Colonel Benjamin Platt had ordered seemed to be working, though CariAnne would need to take it for another ten days.

"Nice column today," Julia said, setting aside the folded *Washington Post* and grabbing her cruller.

"Careful, you're starting to sound like a fan."

Julia stopped short of telling her that she intended to be a fan for a very long time.

A news alert came over the television screen and both mother and daughter shushed her even though Julia wasn't talking. She smiled and simply took her seat.

Julia saw Mary Ellen Wychulis take the podium. She didn't look the least bit uncomfortable replacing her boss. Her new title appeared in a graphic below: Undersecretary of the Food Safety and Inspection Service. If Julia didn't know better she would have thought the woman had been in this position for years.

Wychulis explained what they believed had happened in last week's outbreaks at two separate schools. A supplier for the National School Lunch Program had not reported an internal contamination before shipping out ground beef. She insisted that all the ground-beef products were being recalled and to be on the safe side, no ground beef would be used in school lunches for the next several weeks.

Julia was impressed, although she thought the tall, willowy woman who used to be Benjamin Platt's wife sounded too much like an easily manipulated government employee. An opportunist who was ready to step up, maybe even step over whomever she needed to, all in the name of business as usual.

Remembering that late-night meeting with the USDA, Julia wondered if everything really would be taken care of. Had the real person responsible been caught or would Irene Baldwin be blamed for a contamination that had been in the making long before she even showed up. But that was politics. If Julia remembered correctly, the secretary of agriculture was a crony of the president. Just several days ago the man was more than happy to erroneously blame a poor kitchen worker for this entire mess.

Julia tried to concentrate on the press conference. Wychulis was saying that she wouldn't take any questions.

Of course, they won't take any questions.

But then Wychulis told the crowd of reporters that she would introduce the person who would. The administration's newest cabinet member. The president had just made the appointment official this morning to replace his longtime friend, who was suddenly retiring.

"No," Wychulis insisted, it had nothing to do with this latest recall effort. The timing was totally coincidental.

Then she waved to someone at her left and introduced the new secretary of agriculture: Irene Baldwin.

SEVENTY

Several hundred people had crowded into the small church and yet when Maggie entered she could swear all eyes were watching her. She tried to hide her surprise at seeing Johnny Bosh laid out in his casket right inside the entrance. He looked peaceful in a blue suit and red necktie. Then she saw the football tucked in beside him and the earbuds, the cord and iPod tucked into his pocket. Suddenly she felt tears threatening to well up.

Five teenagers were dead. It was too big a toll for any community. They'd be having funerals all week. She made herself go to this one, despite Lucy's insistence that she stay in bed and get some rest. Griffin had grazed her scalp. It'd leave a scar under her hair—that is when her hair grew back. Today she was able to cover most of the stitches by parting her hair on the opposite side.

She had two broken ribs, some scrapes, and plenty of bruises, but she had been through worse in the past. The physical wounds would heal, adding a few more scars. The rest she would try and tuck into a new compartment in her mind. Later there would be plenty of time for rest. Kunze was giving her the week off. There had been no lecture, no punishment, no suspension—in fact, no explanation other than to tell her he didn't want to see her until the following week. She didn't want to think about how much Kunze may have known about the cattle mutilations when he sent her to the Sandhills. No one would probably ever know the whole story.

As it turned out, Mike Griffin wasn't just an engineer. After Desert Storm he signed on with the U.S. Department of Defense and became a bioengineer. But several years ago he left to work for a Chicago-based research firm. His new employer had contracted with the federal government to use the field house for growing, testing, and developing hybrid strains. The project seemed harmless, so why did Griffin and Frank Skylar go so far to keep Griffin's stepdaughter and her friends away?

"I just wanted to scare them" was what Griffin had told Maggie. But he didn't explain why. Nor would he explain the huge tanks inside the field house that were filled with floating bovine parts, how those parts had gotten there, or what they were being used for. Despite the tanks, Maggie realized that there would probably never be enough evidence to connect Griffin and his employer to the cattle mutilations, but she suspected Wesley Stotter's fantastic story about black ops helicopters and secret government testing may not have been so crazy after all.

Griffin's boots matched the prints left at the scene and in the hospital. He was being charged with attempted murder of Dawson and Maggie. Both he and Skylar were being questioned in the deaths of Kyle and Trevor as well as Wesley Stotter.

Dawson Hayes had told Maggie that the teens had wanted to film their drug-induced experience for YouTube, however no camera had been found by investigators. Late Sunday evening the video had shown up on YouTube. State and federal investigators were still trying to find who posted it. The grainy quality made it impossible to identify anyone but it caught the laser rifle in action and explained the light show the teenagers had experienced.

The smell of burning incense filled Maggie's nostrils, bringing her back to the present. Inside the huge double doorway she caught a glimpse of old women, a group of about a dozen with their heads bent, fingers holding rosary beads, lips barely moving as they led the congregation in prayer. Maggie remembered little of the service, which included processions, lighting of candles, and hymns sung by a choir of Johnny's classmates.

Sitting between Donny Fergussen and Lucy Coy, she tried to close her mind off as she gazed at the stained-glass windows. The morning sunlight burned through the orange and red and purple stained glass, transferring rainbows of color onto the walls. She couldn't help thinking about the irony of how this tragedy had started with a light show and would now end with one.

As for Courtney and Nikki and Johnny—Maggie believed they were victims of Amanda's bullying. She was the one—not Johnny—who had staged the drug parties. It was her way of controlling anyone she wanted to keep in her life and getting rid of those she did not. Donny Fergussen had also found text messages between Courtney, Nikki, and Amanda just seconds before the car crash.

Maggie glanced across the aisle at Dawson and his father. He still looked pale and weak. She wished she could pack up Dawson and send him somewhere safe.

Lucy had asked her to stay for a few days and Maggie had agreed. Last night when she talked to Platt he sounded worried about her injuries, the doctor trying to take care of his patient. He'd even asked to talk to Lucy to make sure Maggie was being taken care of. But Maggie didn't want to be his patient. She didn't know how to tell him that all she really wanted was for him to be with her. Just the thought of it seemed too needy, too vulnerable, and she ended up telling Platt that she was fine, that she'd see him when she got back to D.C. at the end of the week. She explained that it'd take her a couple of days to drive back. She had already decided that Jake would be going with her and they would not be flying.

As the crowd filed out of the church Maggie was grateful for the fresh air. The incense had made her head swim a bit.

She felt Lucy holding on to her elbow and instead of telling her she was fine, Maggie allowed the woman to pamper her. They moved aside and stayed on the portico letting the others go down the steps first, waiting for the crowd to thin. From above they could watch.

It wasn't until Lucy nudged her that Maggie saw him standing across the street. Benjamin Platt waved and made his way through the people getting into cars that were lined up on both sides.

"He's more handsome than I imagined," Lucy told her.

He bounded up the stairs, carefully weaving against the last of the crowd. As he introduced himself to Lucy his eyes flickered over Maggie's battered face. She wanted to tell him she didn't need him coming all this way just to take care of her. That she was fine. Before she could say anything he kissed her, carefully and gently, but leaving Maggie breathless and with little doubt as to whether he thought of her as a patient.

"I thought you and Jake might like some company on the drive home." Platt smiled and added, "But I have to warn you, I love show tunes."

SEVENTY-ONE

―――――

CHICAGO

Roger Bix arrived before noon at the processing center on the north side of Chicago. It was only forty-eight hours since he and Platt had visited the site. This time, however, he brought a fleet of federal marshals in three black SUVs.

They drove single file to the far end of the processing plant's parking lot and pulled up to the chain-link fence.

Immediately Bix knew something was wrong.

The security hut was dark. There was no one to stop their entry.

At first glance, the building appeared abandoned. The enclosed walkway that connected the facility to the processing plant was empty of military personnel, workers, and armored vehicles.

Bix's team waited for the marshals to get out of the SUVs. Then Bix led them into the building. There was no one to greet them in the lobby. The halls were dark and deserted, as were the rooms and laboratories. There were no men and women in white lab coats, no digital microscopes, no computers or rows of monitors. No Philip Tegan. No one. The entire facility had been stripped and was now completely empty.

ACKNOWLEDGEMENTS

———

Special thanks to:

First and foremost, my readers. Your continued and loyal support allows me to do what I love.

My friends Sharon Car, Marlene Haney, Sandy Rockwood, and Patricia Sierra, who keep me grounded and sane and have done so since the beginning of this wonderful crazy journey.

Author Patricia Bremmer and her husband, Martin, for being my eyes and ears on the western front. I'm so glad you didn't get arrested while settting up mock crime scenes in the middle of the Nebraska National Forest.

Dan Frodsham, Rec Tech, and Bob Fetters, Forest Rangers at the Nebraska National Forest, for providing maps and answers. I only hope I did our incredible forest justice, and please forgive my creative license in moving and changing things around.

Melissa Connor, Associate Professor and Forensic

Science Program Director at Nebraska Wesleyan University, along with her students: Jeff Rathman, Kimberly Van Den Akker, Nikki Brophy, Amanda Ruzicka, Leron West, and Kody Connelly. They took an entire afternoon out of their busy schedules to help film a video at NWU's Crime Scene House for my website. And Melissa, thanks also for giving me some ideas on how to process a crime scene outdoors as well as some insight into the Nebraska coroner system. Our conversations are always so morbidly enlightening.

Gary Plank, Assistant Professor at Nebraska Wesleyan University and retired criminal investigator and behavior profiler for the Nebraska State Patrol Investigative Services Division, for answering my questions about the State Patrol and crime scene jurisdictions.

Annie Belatti, whose vast experiences as a trauma nurse and nurse anesthetist provided invaluable information about electrocution and what it might be like to get wrapped up in barbed wire.

Leigh Ann Retelsdorf, Nebraska District Court Judge and retired Douglas County prosecutor, who usually helps me murder my victims, this time was able to access her incredible resume that includes biologist. Thanks for sharing some interesting tidbits about the Nebraska National Forest's diverse wildlife.

The real Mary Ellen Wychulis for her generous donation to the National MS Society and for allowing me to concoct a fictional character in her name. The real Mary Ellen has never, to my knowledge, worked for the USDA, and any resemblance would be a matter of coincidence.

My amazing team at Doubleday, headed by my editor, Phyllis Grann. Special thanks also to Judy Jacoby for your endless attention to detail and caring for each book as if it were your only one.

Also the crew at Little, Brown UK: Catherine Burke and David Shelley.

Ray Kunze, again, for lending his name to Maggie's new boss. Ray had no idea what he was getting into when he asked to be in a novel. And again for the record, the real Ray Kunze is a gentleman and all-around great guy who would never send Maggie to the Nebraska Sandhills to investigate cattle mutilations.

The booksellers, book buyers, librarians, reviewers, and bloggers across the country for mentioning and recommending my novels.

My apologies to the residents of the Nebraska Sandhills and North Platte for my taking some liberty with geography and places such as the Great Plains Regional Medical Center, which, to my knowledge, does not include near as many floors and stairwells as Maggie maneuvered down.

Last, thank you to the ranchers, farmers, and food producers of this nation, who not only do an amazing job of feeding us but of making sure our food is safe. After the spinach recall in 2006, growers and producers got together and developed a safer, more efficient and effective system to curtail future contaminations. They did this on their own and long before the federal government had finished its official investigation.

As I finished the edits to this novel in December 2010, Congress was passing a new food safety bill in response to the egg recall of August/September. Ironically, this massive overhaul of FDA regulations does not extend to the USDA, which oversees beef, poultry, and, yes, eggs.